5
THE
CASCADIA
COUNTY
SERIES

BEHIND *the* Pine

T.J. DEAL

ISBN: 979-8-9907007-7-2

Cover design by: Sarah Hansen © Okay Creations

Editing: Sam Moon

Proofreading: Matthew Deal

Contents

Reader Advisory

This novel contains scenes depicting intense emotional and physical confrontations that may be distressing to readers.

To the audacious and badass women who carry their fears, their anxiety, and their scars, yet refuse to let these shadows overshadow their strength.

Prologue

Maisie

Ethan returns to Three Sisters… with a baby.

Seven Years After Graduation—

What do you do when your world comes crashing down with the mere opening of a door?

Put your big girl panties on, lace up your sneakers, and go for a run. That's what I keep telling myself will help clear my mind after last night. Yet despite repeating that mantra for every other task today, here I am, mid-afternoon, and nothing has worked. Not my early arrival at the coffee hut, scrubbing the floors and appliances before our 5 a.m. opening, nor the meticulous triple-checking of the inventory. Not even the baking of cupcakes, cookies, and a few savory treats could distract me. The countless faces I greeted and served passed by me unnoticed. I've been on the verge of tears all morning—so much so that my sole employee finally sent me home.

I've owned my coffee hut for the last four years—a dream my parents helped me achieve when they assisted me in buying it from the previous owner at twenty-one. Back then, it was just a drive-thru coffee hut with only my friends as customers. I started working there at sixteen, likely logging more hours than I was legally allowed, and became the manager at eighteen. The prices were outrageous, and the coffee brand wasn't great, but I did my best to draw in customers. When the previous owner announced he was selling, it felt like a blessing; I knew I could make something special out of it. And boy, did I. Once I began selling baked goods as well, it became the busiest place in town—no small feat considering we have a major franchise competitor that could easily dominate the small industry.

She wasn't wrong to send me home; I was a mess, and there was no reason for me to hover over her now that the Sunday morning rush had passed. I'd be lying if I said I wasn't disappointed, though. Maisie's has always been my favorite escape, a place where I can lose myself in the grind. Normally, I can tune out the noise, bake treats, and greet customers with a smile. But today was different; it felt like my heart was breaking over and over again each time I pictured Ethan standing in my friend Olivia's doorway with a baby.

Ethan, my Ethan, the best friend I ever had, who I haven't been able to face in years. Carrying not just a baby, but his baby. Talk about the gut punches of all gut punches. I hadn't even known he was seeing someone, let alone that she was pregnant. His parents didn't say anything, neither did any of our mutual friends, yet he definitely walked in with a baby and said "this is my Jake."

So rather than face the heartbreak head on, I did what I do best. I bailed. I couldn't face him or the injustice I felt. I had to leave, to get out of there before he saw me and the devastation written on my face. Even though it's completely undeserved and I'm the villain in this story. *Apparently, I am still the coward I've been since graduation night.*

Thankfully my friend Charlie was there to whisk me out of the party and sneak me out the side door. I felt terrible leaving her "re-do twenty-first" birthday party like that, but I knew I couldn't stay another second.

Which is understandable, right? He was my best friend. We'd been close since second grade—him, me, and our friend Olivia.

But Ethan and I were always linked in a different way. That bond changed on graduation night, when life shifted for me—and I couldn't even bring myself to tell him about it.

A few days later, he left for college, heading straight to Oklahoma to play D1 football. He was drafted into the NFL only part way through his college career with an insane rookie contract. I've followed his journey closely—maybe too closely, if I'm being honest. It's become my dirty secret, my guilty pleasure: the one vice I can't seem to give up.

Even though I had to push him away, I'll always love him.

Of course, he's come back to town to visit his family since then, but I've always managed to be conveniently busy or disappear altogether—even closing down Maisie's for a few days if I couldn't find anyone to cover my shifts.

I reached a point where I realized I couldn't keep losing money. So, I asked Luke, my cousin who works for the Sheriff's department, to tell Ethan to leave me alone. It felt like finality—the last nail in the coffin, my last resort to avoid him, but it worked.

I hadn't seen Ethan in person in nearly seven years. I have no idea if he's dating someone, married, or if his favorite drink is still strawberry milk. I don't know anything about him anymore. And while that may be my doing, it's not something I wished for; it's simply the only way I know how to keep my secret.

Even now, less than a handful of people know what

happened, and I want to keep it that way. No, I need to keep it that way. Which means I'll continue to avoid him. And run.

My feet hit the dirt road, and I sink into the feeling—it's one of the few things I do purely for myself these days. Maisie's consumes most of my life, and while my customers have become friends, I rarely have the chance to connect with them outside of work. But running is different; I've always carved out time for it.

The ranch where my parents live spans a few hundred acres, and my dad has been working for the owner, Will, since he was a teenager himself. This dirt road has witnessed countless runs throughout my life, winding past hay fields and up the hills toward my favorite lookout spot. From there, I can see for miles—taking in the entire ranch, the hardworking hands, the cattle grazing, and the wildlife going about their routines undisturbed.

It's peace, my comfort spot, and the place I do my best thinking. Which is precisely why I drove ten minutes from my own apartment, venturing out of town for this moment of solitude.

As I lose myself in thought, the sound of tires crunching on the dirt road catches my attention. A brand new white F150 approaches, one that I don't recognize as belonging to any of the other ranch hands. Will is always hiring new guys, so it could be one of them—or perhaps it's old man Will himself, always eager to show off his latest shiny pickup.

I move over to the far left side, hoping the dust will settle the other way and I won't end up inhaling most of it with my heaves.

Only the truck slows to a near crawl, stopping right next to me.

The driver being no other than the man I've been running from. Ethan.

He rolls his window down, looking at me with sad eyes that only make me feel more guilty than I knew possible

"Go away, Ethan," I say, turning my back to him as I walk toward the lookout. I shouldn't be surprised he found me out here; this is where we spent countless hours together—daydreaming, sharing secrets, and losing ourselves in conversation beneath the wide-open sky.

But instead of respecting my wish, I hear the unmistakable sound of his door opening as he climbs out.

"Maisie! What the hell? Seven years of a grudge isn't long enough?!" His voice carries through the air, louder than I've ever heard him shout.

"Guess not!" I reply, my heart racing as I resist the urge to turn around.

"That's it? You threw away a lifetime friendship and won't tell me why? Aren't even going to say anything about me having a son?" My knees nearly buckle with guilt. It's all my fault, and I can't even tell him why.

With a deep breath, I slowly turn around to face him. It's like seeing a completely new version of him—somehow taller and more filled out than I remembered. The years of professional training have transformed his physique, adding strength and confidence to his stance. Yet, despite the changes, he's still Ethan. His hair, still a touch too long for most people's liking around here, only makes me want to run my fingers through it, just like I used to.

Right now, the green ring around his iris stands out prominently against the brown inner ring as he glares at me with a mix of rage and sorrow.

"Congratulations, Ethan." The words feel heavy on my tongue, a bittersweet mixture of joy and heartache. "I am truly so happy that you are happy, and successful, and have started your own little family. But please, leave me alone."

He winces, and I catch a flash of pain in his eyes—just an instant, but it cuts deeper than I expected. He shakes his head slowly, as if trying to process the weight of my words. Then he turns, retreating to his truck, and the sound of the door closing feels like a finality, echoing in the air between us.

He rolls down his window as he pulls up next to me, the engine idling softly. "You'll have to find a new place to run if you want to avoid me." His voice barely covers the crack of disappointment beneath it. He gestures toward the lookout. "We're building a house there."

We? I nearly choke on my gasp, the shock striking me like a blow. "But how? It's part of the ranch!"

"He sold it to me." His tone is steady, but there's an undercurrent of frustration that rumbles beneath the surface, something tangled in his chest that he's holding back. As he drives past, I catch sight of the baby carrier in the backseat, a stark reminder of everything that's changed.

I watch the truck drive for so long I see it crest the hill. Our hill. The one that's no longer ours, but his. Theirs.

***

The Day Before Graduation—

As I settled onto the familiar patch of rocks on the hill overlooking the ranch, I watched Ethan's old truck rumble down the dirt road toward me, the setting sun casting a golden glow behind him. Tomorrow marked our graduation day, a milestone cloaked in excitement but tinged with a looming sense of loss for me. I had always pictured this moment differently—a celebration of our future together—but now it felt like we were standing on the edge of two diverging paths: me staying, and him leaving.

I turned just in time to see him jogging up from where he had parked, a warm smile on his face as he called out, 'My fierce Mais!' It's always 'My fierce Mais,' or 'My sour Mais,' or 'My sweet Mais,' depending on the situation, but no matter what, he's called me 'My Mais' for as long as I can remember.

"Hey!" His hair was already ruffled by the wind, likely from driving with his window down. He plopped down beside me. "You ready for tomorrow?"

He grinned that crooked smile that made my heart flutter. "You have no idea. Finally done walking those dusty halls! Then training begins next week, along with a few summer classes." His enthusiasm was palpable, but beneath it lingered an unsteady current in my chest.

"I'm happy for you," I said, forcing a smile even as a wave of melancholy washed over me. "But it's kind of weird, right? Leaving everything behind?" Leaving me.

Ethan chuckled softly. "So weird. But it's the dream, right? Play college ball, hopefully get drafted, make enough money to come back here."

"You really think you'll end up back in Three Sisters?"

"Of course I will," he said, his voice brimming with certainty. "It's home. And—" He hesitated, his expression shifting as he looked out at the horizon.

"And what?" I prompted, my heart racing.

"Where you are," he replied softly. "I've got some big plans —ten-year plans," he added, turning to face me, his captivating rich brown eyes encircled by a green ring, locking onto mine.

"Ten years?" I echoed, my voice barely above a whisper.

"Yep."

The sun sank lower now, painting the sky with brilliant shades of orange and purple. A silence settled between us, my thoughts racing with questions about his plan and why he wasn't elaborating. Would it include me? Even though I would be staying here, going to community college while he was leaving?

"Do you ever think about... us?" I asked suddenly, the words spilling out before I could stop myself.

He looked surprised at my question but intrigued, his brow furrowing slightly. "Us? Like friends?"

"No, I mean... more than friends." I took a shaky breath, willing myself to keep going. "We've always been there for each other. And with you leaving... I guess I just don't know where that leaves us."

Ethan's expression softened, and for a moment, we just stared at each other, the weight of unspoken words hanging between us. I could see the flicker of realization cross his features.

"Honestly, I've thought about it a lot," he confessed, his voice quiet. "In my ten-year plan, I see... you."

My heart raced at his admission, a mix of hope and fear surging within me. "Really?"

"Yeah," he said, shifting closer. "I see the house you've spent years telling me you'd build in this spot, the kids running around—though I'm not sure I'm sold on the Highland cows yet. But everything else? All those stars you wished on out here with me? I want you to have them all. I want to be the one to give them to you."

As he spoke, a wave of emotions washed over me.

"But the best way for me to give you that is to leave," Ethan continued, his eyes serious. "Even if I don't get drafted, I have a full ride to a damn good school. I can get a solid degree and then come back to figure things out."

"You don't think being so far away will change everything? I'm staying here, working the same job with the same people. You'll be off with an entire new team, new friend group, new everything." The insecurities bubbled to the surface, and I struggled to mask them with carefully chosen words.

His gaze locked onto mine, filled with sincerity and admiration, as if he truly believed that distance and time apart wouldn't change a thing. "Not sure anything could change how much you mean to me, Mais. You've always been 'My Maisie.' You mean too much to me for me to mess this up. We trust each other, right? I'd never do anything to hurt you."

It feels like we should've had this talk ages ago, especially since we've been tiptoeing around the fact that we don't date anyone else and spend all our free time together. I might worry about what's coming next, but I trust him completely; I'd never do anything to hurt him either. Still, there's this nagging thought in the back of my mind—what if something happens that changes everything between us? Could I ever truly move on from him?

Chapter One

Maisie

Present Day—

*B*uzz. Buzz. Buzzzzzz.* My alarm began the frantic vibrations on the wood bedside table, jolting me out of a peaceful sleep. My arm flung out to silence the horrendous rhythmic noise. Three a.m. comes far too early every morning, but just the thought of opening the best drive-through coffee hut in town is enough to pull me from the comfort of my dreams. That, and if I don't get up right this second, I won't have time to brush my teeth, hair, and put on enough makeup to cover the dark circles under my eyes from never getting enough sleep.

I've owned Maisie's for nearly a decade now, and I love it more and more each day. The routine, owning a successful business, being a prominent part of the community around here—all of it has been a lifeline for me. The one thing to keep me grounded and sane.

As I made my way down the quiet streets, the cool morning air was filled with the sweet scent of pine and the promise of a new day. Streetlights illuminate the rustic buildings of a town known for its 1880s style charm. Flower pots adorn the entirety of Main Street, and it's not lost on me that I grew up in the most beautiful small town in Oregon.

It's still too early for most of the town to be awake, but I know that later this summer, there will be a few stragglers lingering, hanging onto the night. For now, though, I cherish my morning walks in the brisk early summer air, grateful that my tiny apartment is just a few blocks away.

Maisie's sits on the edge of town, in the parking lot of our only grocery store. Luckily, it has its own cozy lot, framed by pine trees and vibrant shrubs that give a sense of seclusion. The warm, rustic wood siding, along with custom metal signs and carved wood details, create the chic Western vibe I had always envisioned.

Once inside, I flipped on the lights and took a moment to breathe in the familiar aromas of coffee grounds and baked goods that linger in the air seemingly permanently. The coffee hut may look small on the outside, but it's surprisingly spacious on the inside. A few years ago, I upgraded the entire building and dedicated half of the space to a full kitchen, ensuring I had room to bake without getting in my barista's way while they handled customers and standard coffee orders.

With two ovens radiating warmth, shelves filled with sprinkles and flour, and a sturdy mixer ready for dough, this space feels as much like home as my small apartment—maybe even more so.

I set my things down and glanced at the clean workspace before me. My first task was staring right at me: deciding what to bake. Usually, that's an easy call—I plan and think about it days in advance. But this year, I underestimated how many we'd go through and had to scramble yesterday to bake more. Luckily, I don't have to worry much about my savory items.

The bagels, croissants, and other goodies are delivered fresh by Ralph, a local vendor whose wife, Gail, bakes with a magic I could never replicate.

With the rodeo in town and a flood of out-of-towners hitting the drive-through for their morning fix, I knew I had to be on top of my game—that meant doubling my usual recipes. After we closed yesterday, I spent the evening in the kitchen, prepping for the busy days ahead. I dedicated three hours to making the dough for light, fluffy brioche cinnamon rolls, which I let rise overnight. They always turn out buttery and sweet—an undeniable crowd favorite.

Next up were the chocolate cookies. I normally keep a sizable stash of pre-made dough in the freezer—such a lifesaver on hectic days like yesterday and potentially today. Which means, I'll be using the entire batch I had waiting, along with the peanut butter cookie dough right beside it.

Finally, I settled on raspberry muffins topped with a crunchy streusel. The tart berries and sweet, crumbly topping are sure to tempt even the pickiest customers. Plus, one of my top customers—my 'Little Razz'—always shows up on Fridays, and I know raspberries are his favorite.

As I finished sprinkling cinnamon sugar over the dough and prepped the trays, I got caught up in the rhythm. In what felt like a blink, the door swung open—and in walked Ashleigh, my barista. It was only 5 a.m., but she already looked like she was channeling her inner Kacey Musgraves. Short shorts, rhinestone cowgirl boots, fluttery top—gorgeous as always.

I look down at myself, noting the dusting of flour covering my jeans and sweatshirt.

"Good morning!" She sing-songs as she tosses her purse in the cabinet.

"Hello, looo-vely! How do you always look like you're ready for a date and not about to serve coffee all morning long?"

"How do you think I'm going to *get* that date? Someday a hot, rich, man is going to drive-thru and love my macchiato so much he has to come back and get my number!"

"You want a man that drinks a macchiato?"

"I just want *a* man. What he likes to drink isn't really my business." *If only it were that simple...*

"Well, you're going to have 'em lining up today with those shorts."

"Good. Maybe I'll find myself a nice cowboy." The familiar jingle of a car approaching makes us both glance out the window. Not surprisingly, it's Cooper, Leo, and Delta—the newcomers to town, early risers, almost always coming through before heading to work for the Elite Forces Security and Contracting company my friend Hayes started.

"Not a cowboy," she says with a smirk, "but a fine-ass Navy SEAL. Even better." She shimmy-shimmies her shoulders and flashes a huge, dazzling smile. "Bright and early—just how I like 'em. What can I get y'all?"

Delta's behind the wheel, fingers tapping on the steering wheel as he fights the urge to sneak a look at my young barista when she turns to start their order. I've got a feeling he's holding back because of the age gap—I'm guessing he's probably in his early thirties, maybe a little older. Which, knowing Ash, wouldn't be such a big deal. She's definitely old enough to drink, so the age difference wouldn't really matter—not to her, anyway.

Cooper, on the other hand, doesn't even attempt to hide his attraction. His mustache curls into a lopsided grin as he leans over Delta to ask, "Ash, why you looking so gorgeous before the sun even rises?"

That's my cue. I lean forward enough for them to see me standing there. "Cooper, whatever your full name is, are you seriously shooting your shot before the sun's even up?"

"Agreed," Delta mutters, shoving Cooper back to his side with a firm hand. His broad shoulders stretch against his black shirt, muscles rippling beneath ink that snakes up his arms and peeks out from beneath his collar. He looks like he's been carved from stone—heavy, tattooed, and dangerous in a silent, compelling way. His buzz cut emphasizes the sharpness of his jawline, and his piercing gaze flicks toward Ashleigh with an almost quiet intensity. *Ooh, Delta definitely has a thing for my barista.*

From the back, Leo's loud laugh draws my attention. He might be the best looking of the group—neatly styled hair that's clearly freshly combed, deep-set blue eyes, that classic Hollywood charisma thing. Yet, he doesn't really do it for me. Sure, he's beautiful and, according to my friend Odessa, interested in me, but he's never actually made a move. And truth be told, I don't get butterflies around him. Not like I do with ... well, someone I'd rather not think about right now.

"Maisie, you coming to the rodeo tonight?" Cooper asks, snapping me out of my thoughts.

"Not tonight. I'll be there tomorrow though!" I reply a little too chipper—Odessa's been pestering me about coming along, and I couldn't think of an excuse. Now, I kind of wish I had.

"No shit?" Cooper grins, glancing back at Leo. "We'll all be there then. Maybe Leo here can buy you a drink and maybe even take you for a spin on the dance floor."

Before I can reply, Leo's hand flashes out—so fast I barely see it—smacking Cooper on the back of the head and pushing him into Delta. Delta responds instantly, shoving Cooper back with a stern look.

"Here you go, *boys*," Ashleigh announces, handing over their black coffees with a playful smile.

"See ya tomorrow, pretty girl." Leo says with so much suave in his tone that I instantly feel my knees go a little shaky. I can have my head in the clouds quite a bit, but did I miss something? Never, ever, has Leo been so brazen—or never have I noticed. *Do I like it? Maybe.*

Delta starts to pull away, and all I can do is smile and wave, words still caught in my throat from Leo being flirty.

Ashleigh turns toward me, grinning like the Cheshire Cat. "Damn, girl! Leeeeooo? That man is all things fine."

"Yes, he is..." and I should be over the moon about the attention, but it doesn't feel right.

"Then... Why do you look like you just tried to solve a Rubik's Cube blindfolded?"

I glance at her and see the genuine curiosity on her face. How do I explain that I'm still hung up on my first crush, even though I know I'll never be able to have him because I'm hiding a secret I'm too scared to share? It's been on my mind for months—how to move past the guilt and be friends with him. The problem is, I don't know where to start or how to let him go completely, or even how to just be his friend anymore.

Thankfully, I don't have to answer. Another car pulls up, and the rest of the morning drags us into full swing.

Chapter Two

Ethan

Standing in the sleek kitchen of the Ponderosa Pine, I catch my reflection in the stainless-steel fridge. The man staring back isn't just a former NFL star who once lit up stadiums; he's also a father, a business owner, and a man *still* tethered to his past in ways that seem unfathomable. *How the hell did that happen?*

When I found out I was going to be a dad, everything changed instantly. Just days away from signing a new contract and committing another four years of my life to football, one knock on my door changed it all. From that point on, there was no question in my mind—I couldn't let my child be raised by a nanny.

I had seen it too often among NFL players: their wives became the backbone that holds everything together, and without them many players struggled to juggle their careers and family life. That wasn't the life I wanted for my child. Raised by a nanny, or multiple, while I lived a dream I wasn't even sure I wanted to begin with. No. I wanted him to grow up surrounded by family, friends, and community.

Staring into those tiny eyes that matched my own, I knew I made the right decision to walk away from football. Which is how I found myself back in my small hometown, trading the adrenaline of the game for the boy I had barely met but already realized I needed more than I thought possible.

Even six years later, I don't regret the decision for a second. I have a healthy son who is the miniature version of me in every way, down to the above average height and goofy laugh. While doing it alone has been challenging, and definitely not the life I had planned, my parents have been my rock, supporting me every step of the way. And my best friend Olivia has been a blessing, too. Her youngest is just a few months older than Jake, and they've been best friends since the beginning.

A loud crash behind me jolts me back to reality. I turn around to find Chef Julian—famous as the best chef in Central Oregon—staring at me with his trademark eccentric look. Tall and skinny, covered in tattoos of swirling kitchen stuff—whisks, flames, vintage knives—that seem to wind across his skin. His piercing gaze and commanding presence hit me like a ton of bricks, making me realize I've just been standing there, lost in my reflection. He grins at me with a look that clearly says, 'stop staring at yourself and get the fuck out of my kitchen.'

"Sorry, Chef," I mumble, scratching the back of my neck.

He waves it off. "If I wasn't so rigid about keeping my kitchen in pristine condition, maybe people wouldn't get so distracted..."

I laugh. "What's the special tonight?"

He launches into details, tossing around technical terms that go over my head—things like mesclun and effiler—and I nod along, pretending to understand. Honestly, I trust whatever he's cooking up will be incredible, even if I haven't got a clue what half of it means.

"Can't wait to try it. I'll be around if you need anything," I say, even though I know he probably won't. I step back, letting Julian do his thing in the kitchen.

The restaurant is quiet now—just me and a few staff members working this shift. Kade and Janet are the only servers on duty, both seasoned pros who know the ins and outs of running the floor smoothly. CJ, a young barback I recently brought on, is in the kitchen catching up on dishes from the lunch rush with Julian's crew. This lull in the action feels like a much-needed breather before the rodeo crowd hits later—when the doors will burst open, and the place will become a madhouse.

I trust Callie, my manager, to handle that rush. She used to be the best bartender we had, and I know she's got the experience to step in wherever she's needed. It's easier for me to avoid the chaos altogether, especially with the out-of-town visitors eager to catch a glimpse of "Ethan Flacco, the highest-paid rookie and former Vikings quarterback." They come searching for stories, trying to mingle, but I've got little interest in that version of myself anymore.

As I prepare the "ready station"—cutting limes, refilling ingredients—I can't help but drift back to the past, to her. Maisie. My incredible, loving, fierce Maisie. She was never just a best friend, even though we both tried to hide the feelings for years. And then, practically the day after we finally admitted them, she stopped talking to me. Hasn't spoken to me since, and honestly, it still stings like hell. Why? What the hell could have happened to make her go from loving me to hating me so quickly? I've gone over every detail of both nights, trying to piece together what went wrong. Talked to everyone we know, but no one knows anything—or they won't tell me.

Even after all these years, I still can't shake the feelings I have for her. I've tried to move on—becoming a single dad to Jake, messing around with a few fleeting out-of-town flings—

nothing serious. But no matter what, Maisie's always in the back of my mind, lurking in the corners of my heart.

The door swings open, and the soft chime of the restaurant bell pulls me from my thoughts. I push aside the familiar ache, reminding myself that my life is more than a lingering past—I've got Jake, my family, and a successful business to focus on.

"Ethan!" My friend Odessa bursts in, all six feet tall, long legs and the brightest blonde hair you've ever seen. Back in the day, neither of us would have expected to end up in the same town, but she was a supermodel with connections that ran parallel to mine. She used to joke that we were "friend soulmates"—the kind who wasn't romantic, but somehow just meant to be friends, no matter what life throws at you. I don't exactly subscribe to that notion, but I get where she's coming from. If I really believed in soulmate stuff, I'd say I already found mine—she just seems to have completely forgotten it.

"Hey, Dess. Avoiding the rodeo crowd?"

"Exactly what I'm doing!" She glances around, surveying the mostly empty restaurant. "Luke's been working fourteen-hour days, and I just didn't have the energy to go tonight, so I called in a to-go order."

I nod, understanding her sentiment. Luke's the sheriff of Cascadia County and pretty much the poster boy for the rodeo. He's not just part of the events—he works the crowd, keeps an eye on the patrons, and watches over his deputies. It's more than a full-time gig, and just thinking about it makes me want a nap.

"Think I'm gonna grab something from here before I head home, too. Don't really feel like cooking for one."

"No Jake tonight?"

"Nope! Movie night with the Turners," I reply, watching Odessa's face fall into a pout at the mention of Olivia and her kids, Ellie and Ben.

"Damn! I should've gone to that. Olivia's pregnancy crav-
ings have been crazy lately—I live for the stuff she makes."

I pretend to gag. "Yeah, she asked for an extra pickle
cheeseburger with chocolate sauce the other day."

Odessa laughs and teases, "You won't believe the last time I
was over, she used strawberry yogurt as a dip for her nacho-
flavored Doritos!"

The swinging door clatters open, and I turn to see CJ
walking out with a tub full of clean dishes. His messy dark hair
hangs over his eyes, and he quickly gives Odessa a nod, flipping
his hair out of his face.

Without saying a word, he wrestles the heavy tub of dish-
ware to the counter, clearly in his own zone where nothing else
seems to matter. Odessa, of course, ignores that and keeps
right on.

"Hey, CJ!" Odessa greets him with way more enthusiasm
than he's given her. "What's that stand for, anyway? 'CJ'?"

"Carter James," he says, the name rolling off his tongue
with an air of calm nonchalance, as if he's completely oblivious
to the impact his name might hold in our small town. I'm sure
he has no idea, being new to town, but we really don't care for
guys named Carter.

Odessa's reaction is immediate; her enthusiasm dims as she
visibly recoils, the playful banter evaporating into a moment of
caution. "Yeah, let's keep that to yourself around here," she
murmurs, casting a wary glance toward me.

"Why's that?" he asks, glancing from me to her, his hands
still occupied.

"Long story," Odessa replies, her tone turning playful.
"Anyway, where you from?"

"Uh," he pauses, then shrugs and says, "kind of all over.
Moved around a lot."

Odessa nods, but just as she opens her mouth to ask

another question, CJ hurriedly puts away the last glass and heads back into the kitchen.

"He's—"

"Quiet?" I finish for her.

"Yep." She shrugs, leaning against the bar. "And he wants to bartend?"

"That's what he says... He's a good kid. Never late, doesn't complain about the crappy shifts." That's an understatement, honestly. He's a top-tier worker, keeps his head down, works extra shifts, and I appreciate that he doesn't get starstruck by Odessa's fame.

She shrugs again, still not convinced. "Hmm. Isn't bartending like thirty percent skill and seventy percent therapist, though?"

"Seems like it," I agree. "Callie's got her eye on him. She'll have him a social butterfly in no time."

"That's true. If anyone can get someone out of their shell, it's her."

Her fingers tap lightly on the shiny pine bar, drawing my attention.

"Sooo—there's actually something else I need to tell you."

"Alright." I set the knife down, bracing myself against the opposite side of the counter. Whenever someone starts a conversation like that, it usually leads to something life altering.

"Maisie is coming to the rodeo with us tomorrow."

"Oh-kay?" I ask, raising an eyebrow. Maisie doesn't typically do group hangouts—she's always swamped with work or avoiding me—but I guess this isn't completely out of the blue.

"And before you freak out, just know I heard this rumor at the gym, so it may not mean anything," she says, lowering her voice and leaning in closer.

"Odessa," I urge, feeling urgency creep into my tone. I can see her hesitate, and my palms start sweating.

Finally, she lets it slip: "Apparently, Leo is making his move. Something about a beer and a dance?"

My jaw tightens, and I clench my teeth without thinking. A flicker of anger sparks inside me, hot and sudden. No one from town has ever dared to go there—especially knowing our history. Everyone around here knows that it was always supposed to be Maisie and I—the family, the house, the happily ever after.

And I was a breath away from having it... until... fuck. Until I don't know what happened.

But, even I have to admit myself: it's gone on for too long.

Chapter Three

Ethan

The Graduation Party

Twelve years prior—

Walking into the gymnasium for our high school graduation felt surreal. The atmosphere hummed with excitement, filled with the sweet smell of candy and popcorn. This year's grad party theme was Las Vegas, and I had to admit, the committee nailed it. The place looked like a vibrant casino, every table draped in green felt and gleaming chips glinting under the lights. Blackjack, poker, and roulette tables lined the space, laughter and shuffling cards filling the air in an intoxicating symphony. Plus, I'm walking in with the most beautiful girl in Three Sisters, and after our conversation last night, I finally feel like we are on the same page.

I had planned on having this big conversation the morning before I left to start summer training—meeting her up on our hill as the sun rose behind us. But, of course, she beat me to it.

Straight up, asking if I'd ever thought about us. Like I hadn't been thinking about an us every single day since I was twelve.

Now, Maisie's on my arm in her stunning gold dress, practically glowing under the colorful lights. Her light-brown hair is pinned up into some fancy updo that I really hope she takes out later. Honestly, I couldn't have planned a better day—standing on stage next to her, the stolen kisses hidden from everyone, and tonight, spending some of my last few hours in town with her.

Her grip tightens around my bicep, her long nails digging in, and I look down to see the biggest smile on her face.

"Are you ready for me to kick your butt at Blackjack?" she teases, her voice bubbling with excitement.

Olivia strolled across the transformed gym toward us, her long legs carrying her with an effortless confidence that I had always admired. Even among the sea of familiar faces, Olivia stood out as slightly taller than the average girl, though I still towered over her, just as I did over Maisie.

I couldn't help but notice Maisie's hand slip from my arm as she spotted Olivia approaching. I lifted an eyebrow in question, but Maisie simply shrugged and smiled, her eyes brightening at the sight of our friend.

"Guys—You'll never believe what happened!" Olivia exclaimed, a wide grin stretching across her face. "Tommy already got kicked out for spiking the punch."

"Idiot." I groan, shaking my head. He played varsity soccer, but last I heard, he wasn't planning on taking it anywhere. Honestly, I have a feeling he'll end up working for his dad's landscaping company for the rest of his life. That thought only solidifies my decision to leave. My dad's always made good money, but I don't want to spend my life working for him. It'll be hell without Maisie, but I wasn't lying about my plan—to become something for her.

The two of them lit up as they talked about what they wanted to do tonight, and I scanned the room, from the game tables to the few people dancing in the center, to the random people on the bleachers. Our graduating class wasn't very big, but it looks like everyone showed up.

They settle on the Blackjack table first, and I follow behind like I always do. Only this time, I can openly stare at Maisie because she knows all my secrets. No more worrying that I'll say too much or fuck it all up because she feels the same.

I sit next to Maisie and it's not lost on me, that it probably doesn't look like anything is different to Olivia. The three of us have our spots, and Maisie has always been in the middle. Not that Olivia and I aren't close, it's just Maisie is the crux between us. Without her, I'm sure we would be friends, but I'm not sure if it'd be the same.

"Alright, graduates, welcome to the Blackjack tables of the future!" Mr. Sanchez, our former physic's teacher, says, puffing up his chest like he's announcing the next big moment of our graduation ceremony. "Tonight, it's all about luck, strategy, and a bit of good ol' teacher bribery. Just kidding—no extra credit for you tonight, but I'll take a good story any day!"

The three of us get lost in the game, laughing at how many times we lose to Mr. Sanchez. He acts completely oblivious, taking his role serious, pretending to be a real Blackjack dealer. I keep checking my watch, though because in the back of my mind I know this night will be over before I want it to.

Leilani, one of Maisie's and Olivia's friends, leans down and whispers something in Olivia's ear and then Maisie's. I watch Olivia's eye's light up, and then Maisie shrugs in response.

"What?" I lean in closer to Maisie and she turns to me, her warm breath sends tingles down my spine, but it's killed when she says, "there's a bonfire after this, want to go?"

"I wish. Mom wants me home early because the Frenches are in town." My mom doesn't normally care about a curfew, but they came up specifically to see my graduation, and I haven't spent much time with them since they got here yesterday. I already had an ear full last night about skipping out to hang out with Maisie, and while it was worth it, I do feel guilty about not seeing our family friends. Alexandra, especially, she feels like a cousin with how close our families have been. We travel to see them often and they come up here most summers.

I see the disappointment written all over her pretty face and wish I could take back the words.

"Oh..."

"You and Liv should go, though. Don't let my lameness ruin your night." My shoulder bumps into her, and I let it settle there.

"I—"

"Please, Maisie! It sounds like everyone is going out there. I'm not even going to drink. We'll just hang out for a bit."

Reluctantly, she agrees, but something about it feels off—like she shouldn't go without me. It's a feeling I know I'll have to get used to if we're going to make this long-distance thing work.

I place my hand gently on her lower back, trying to offer some reassurance that I'm fine with it. She relaxes into me just as Mr. Sanchez starts dealing the next hand.

She sneaks a glance at her bottom card, and I can feel her tense up. I catch the smile she tries to suppress, barely even glancing at my own cards. I want this win to be all about her.

"So, what's it going to be, future leaders of the world? Are you going to hit it big or stay here forever?"

"Hit," I say just as she exclaims, "Blackjack!" Her excitement bubbles over as she flips her other card, her smile growing wider as the playful banter washes over us.

Mr. Sanchez, sensing the shift in the energy, raises an eyebrow at me, and I just shrug in response. I'm pretty sure he already knows Maisie and I have a thing—and I'm sure he can tell that something's changed between us.

Thirty minutes later, I feel my phone vibrate in my pocket, probably my mom reminding me to get home soon, but I don't check it. Instead, I give myself five more minutes to stay with Maisie.

"I should probably head home soon," I finally admit, reluctant to end the moment.

"Yeah, of course," Maisie says, her voice steady, but I catch the disappointment lingering in her eyes as I pull away. The little pinch in my chest deepens—a bittersweet ache—wishing I could hold her just a little longer.

"But I'll definitely catch up with you tomorrow, alright?" I forced a smile, hoping it would ease the moment, but the prospect of leaving felt heavy.

She nodded and started to pull away, but before she could, I kissed her, not caring who else was around. Hopefully, everyone, and they'd all know the line was crossed and there's no going back.

When I finally let go and backed away, she was at least smiling and laughing.

"Tomorrow then?"

"Lunch on the hill. I'll text you the second I can break free."

Chapter Four

Maisie

"Good morning, Millennials!" The familiar voices of my favorite podcasters blast through my car's radio, and somehow, hearing Jax and Claudia always helps to calm my frayed nerves.

I considered cranking up the volume as I hit the country roads, but frankly, diving into breakup or love songs doesn't feel like the right move for me at the moment. Not when I feel like I'm on the verge of crying or throwing myself a party. A true conundrum, that the 'swirlies' would say I need to get over by getting under someone else. *Or something like that.*

My spiral all started with the little dance and drink Leo suggested this morning—or, really, it was Cooper who put it out there for Leo. Part of me is all about the idea of someone like Leo being brave enough to step over that invisible line Ethan drew with guilt and toxic masculinity, but the bigger part of me is completely freaked out.

It's not because Leo feels unsafe—he definitely doesn't. It's because I feel like I'd be giving him a piece of myself I can't even share with the person I truly want. I'm not clueless; I know Ethan is still waiting for the day I let him back in. But I can't—I can't go back to that night and explain what happened. And without doing that, there's no way we can move forward. And even if we could, what would that look like? I'd just be stuck in the friend zone, watching him fall for someone else? Nope, I'll keep my distance—where my secrets are stuffed so far down inside of me that I hardly even think of them.

So, how can I even think about going out with Leo? I can't. But it wasn't a date—it was a dance... therefore, there wouldn't be talking during a dance, no deep dives into our emotional states, right? *I could do that.*

Each question in my mind only leads to more questions. I've truly never been this indecisive; it feels like I can't make a decision to save my life. It was even affecting my work—I ended up leaving three hours early. Ralph made his delivery just a few minutes after those annoyingly handsome Bod Squad guys left, and I couldn't even choose between mini quiches or tarts for next week's order.

That's how I found myself pulling up to my sister Margie's house—a much-needed escape from the chaos of my emotions. Margie's full name is Marguerite, but she's gone by Margie since her teenage years because no one could pronounce it correctly. She's always been quirky yet conventional—naming her kids rhyming names like Cody, Brody, Jody, and Melody, but keeping them pretty typical.

What really surprises me is that her husband, Jason, actually goes along with it. He's more of a blue-collar tough guy, running his own painting company that keeps him busy with both commercial and residential projects. Despite his long hours and being the primary breadwinner, he somehow always makes time for the kids' games and concerts. I'd give him more credit for that—if we got along better. For some reason, we've just never really clicked on a friend level.

They married pretty quickly—mostly because she got pregnant pretty quickly. Their oldest is now thirteen, and the youngest is seven. Jason's been around since my senior year of high school, but we're not exactly close. If anything, I'd say he earns a solid C- in the marriage department—*and a F in the brother-in-law department.* I spend a lot of time wondering what Margie sees in him—other than him being a decent dad and a somewhat good-looking guy. But, given my current situation, I have no room to judge.

I step inside and am instantly hit with the wild, beautiful chaos of their house. Laughter, arguing, and the occasional crash of something falling meld into a noisy, slightly overwhelming symphony. Luckily, their closest neighbor isn't within earshot. Their house, out in the country not far from my parents, has that classic "perfect country home" vibe—something that, genuinely, feels more like our parents' place than Margie might be willing to admit. Everything's either handmade or bought at an antique store, pieced together in that old-school farmhouse style. It's not really my taste, but it's definitely Margie's— her mismatched color scheme and all.

In my hand, I clutch the pan of still-warm Heath bar cookies, the aroma drifting out of the foil. I wouldn't be surprised if one of the kids is lurking around the corner, ready to jump out and scare me, or about to come barreling through and knock me over.

"Marguerite!" I yell, trying to cut through the madness. "Where you at?"

"In here!" She shouts from what sounds like the kitchen.

I make my way to her and find her perched at her makeshift workspace—their dining room table. The smell of leather fills the air, and although it may not look like much, it's where she creates some of the most incredible handcrafted leather goods—

wallets, belts, bags, you name it. I swear her creativity and talent knows no bounds.

Her head snaps up, glasses sliding down her nose, and her long blonde braid falls slightly over her face as she sniffs the air. "Oh no, are those Heath bars? Who died?!" Okay, so maybe they're my go-to stress-baking cookies.

"No one died. They're Jody's favorite!" And frankly, sometimes you just need that melted chocolate and toffee oozing from each gooey chunk, you know?

The squint in her eyes tells me she's not buying it, but instead of pressing, she asks, "To what do we owe this lovely visit then? You don't normally just drop by unannounced..."

"Can't an aunt bring her niece her favorite treat when she gets all A's on her report card?!"

"Mom call?"

"Yeah, she went on for ten minutes about her perfect grandkids, then gave me a two-minute lecture about how she's just happy you gave her so many since it looks like I'll be celibate for the rest of my life."

"Niiiice. So mom telling you she wants you to get laid is the real reason for the cookies?" *Not exactly.*

I nod noncommittally and set the cookies on her cluttered kitchen counter. Margie's great at a lot of things, but housecleaning isn't exactly one of them—then again, four kids.

I take a seat on the wooden stool, grab a cookie, and turn around to see her already back at work.

As I watch Margie hand-tool a purse, the precision and detail she puts into her work leave me in awe. It looks so professionally done that I can hardly believe it's her own creation. With her talent, I know that once she has a little more time, she could really take her craft even further, but for now, she's maxed out.

"You're making that look so good, I can't even believe you

made this," I say, leaning over her workspace to get a closer look.

She glances up, a smirk playing on her lips. "Uhm, ouch."

I laugh. "You know I didn't mean it like that!"

Margie rolls her eyes playfully. "Whatever. You heard from Liv lately? At eight months pregnant, she's gotta be *miserable* in this heat."

"I know—and it's barely June!"

"At least she's got that hot AF guy waiting on her hand and foot. Seriously, she went from the golden boy Dan Turner to a literal Navy SEAL? She's always been gorgeous and kind, but damn..."

Olivia's late husband, and the father of her other two kids, was killed on duty a few years back. She went through a really dark time before she met Drew, so there's also no one more deserving of a happily ever after than her.

"You're tellin' me. She IS goals landing that one."

Margie leans in closer, her eyes sparkling with mischief. "Heard a rumor those goals aren't that far away for you... Leo?"

Darn this small-town and its gossip!

I hesitate, feeling the words catch in my throat. "Yup. He made plans to meet up. It's just a drink, ya know?"

Her hand hits the table so loud that I cringe backward. "No, I do not know! You haven't had 'a drink' with *anyone*. Ever! And *Leo*? That man looks like he belongs in a Hallmark Christmas movie, not a Navy SEAL."

"Yeah..." I reply, trying to sound nonchalant despite the rush of nerves flooding through me. "But it's probably nothing."

Her expression shifts, and I can see the concern flickering in her eyes. "Okay... and what about Ethan? How do you think that's goin' down?"

I feel my defenses rise instantly. "It'll be fine."

When she doesn't say anything only stares at me with that

eyebrow arch that only moms know how to do, I cave. "We're not together, Margie! We haven't talked in yeeeears."

"I know," she says gently, her tone still probing. "But when are you going to let that go, Maisie?"

"Enough," I snap, feeling a knot tighten in my stomach. "I'm not talking about that."

I know she's one of the few people I confided in about that night. It was only her insistence that pushed me to see a therapist, Helen, and while it helped for a time, it was also a painful process that I never hope to relive.

"I'm only pushing because you're sitting here stuffing cookies into your mouth like the damn Cookie Monster because you got asked out on a date!"

Quickly, I blurted, "It wasn't a date!"

"Fine, fine," she concedes, holding her hands up defensively. I notice the red smear of leather stain on her palm, and a chill runs down my spine as flashes of my own hand, battered and stained the same way, flicker in my mind.

"Not a date," she continues, and I blink—just like that, the image vanishes. I'm back to looking at Margie. "But a man is showing interest in you, and it scares you."

"It does," I admit, even though the words feel stuck in my throat.

She stays quiet again, waiting for me to gather my thoughts and explain. It drives me crazy when she does that, but she's the best at prying—probably because she always capitalizes on my oversharing in moments of quiet.

I don't even know where to start. I've thought about everything all day—from graduation night to this morning with Leo.

"Remember when I called him right after he won that championship?" I finally start, choosing a spot somewhere in the middle of where I should have begun, but I know Margie will catch on. "Helen told me I didn't have to explain anything to Ethan. That I could just tell him I wasn't ready to talk about it, but still let him know I was thinking of him, rooting for him."

She listens silently, her eyes steady.

"I was trying to do that," I go on, voice softening. "But then Alexandra answered, and..." I trail off, frustration bubbling up. "She said stuff that just sent me spiraling right back into that depression." Alexandra, as harsh as she's been, was right— I shouldn't be burdening him with all my mess. And I still have a truckload of it.

"I remember—you stopped seeing Helen after that. You threw yourself into school and work instead," Margie says quietly, giving me a gentle nudge.

"I did. And it saved me in a way. I focused solely on working my way towards Maisie's, and now look where my business is at. But—the things that Alexandra said really stuck with me. It was like she spoke every bad thought I had about myself. I've spent so much time rebuilding myself and my confidence. I'm scared to let anyone tear that down. Letting in Leo feels like a betrayal to Ethan."

Margie sighs, letting the conversation settle for a moment. "I get that. But at some point you need to find peace within yourself and move forward. Maybe letting go of the cold shoulder toward Ethan with help you let go of some of it. I'm not saying be his best friend again, but maybe just raise the white flag."

I can feel the weight of her words pressing against the walls I've built, rattling them like they're trying to get in and convince me it's finally time.

"I'll consider it," I reply, feeling a flicker of uncertainty. "Truthfully, moving on is part of why I agreed to meet Leo in the first place."

"Honey, you'll never move on from Ethan. He was your

first big, all-consuming love... but that doesn't mean you can't move forward without him."

"Yeah..." And for the first time in a very long time, I'm starting to feel like I do want to move forward in life. I've been stuck since graduation night, and it's time to start living again.

"Alright! Enough with the sentimental shit. Let's talk outfits," she says with enthusiasm, switching gears. "You need to wear something that shows off your *ass*-ets but is still comfortable. And just relax! Have fun with Leo. Lots of fun in you know what I mean."

"Your kind of fun resulted in four kids! Think I'll pass on that."

"Meh, only three were fun. One was a quickie that turned into the best surprise."

"Margie!" We both laugh, and the tension begins to lift.

I'm going into tomorrow night with confidence, a fresh-outlook, and if Margie has it her way, a very promiscuous outfit.

Chapter Five

Ethan

"Loooove ya! Bye."

"What are you listening to Dad?" I glance over my shoulder to see Jake bouncing down the hall toward me, already ready to go.

"Nothing, big man. Just a podcast." I chuckle lightly taking note that we are practically twins, wearing nearly matching outfits. Our pearl snap shirts have a subtle floral print, complemented by dark jeans and our best cowboy boots. He's the best mini-me I could have hoped for, capturing the spirit and energy I had when I was his age.

"You ready to go?" I ask. He nods enthusiastically and quickly heads out the front door toward my truck. He climbs into his booster seat and clicks the belt into place, already on cloud nine and probably excited for tonight. Meanwhile, I've been feeling on edge ever since Odessa's big announcement yesterday. I can't shake the worry about seeing Maisie with Leo, and I'm doing my best to keep my composure. To make things a little more complicated, my mom offered to let Jake have a sleepover, so I can enjoy a night out. *Maybe I'll just find an out-*

of-towner buckle bunny and forget about all the stress for a while.

When we arrive at the rodeo, finding parking is a breeze. I wave at a few people we know from around here, and try to avoid small talk as we walk in. Jake is bouncing in place, his excitement palpable as he asks, "Can we get cotton candy right now? Grandma said she'd buy it!"

"Soon, buddy," I tell him, chuckling at how eager he is. My mom has been looking forward to this just as much as he has, and I really love seeing how close they are. The rodeo was one of my favorite childhood memories with her, and I'm glad Jake gets to have that experience too.

As we approach the entrance, I can't help but notice the line, short but packed with energy. My gaze sweeps over the crowd, landing on a group of young girls wearing boots and daisy dukes that seem to cut just a little too high for my comfort. They all giggle and sway, probably having already pregamed in the parking lot. Cringing, I make a mental note to text Callie to remind her to ID everyone—twice. I've learned my lesson; appearances can be deceiving, and I don't want anyone slipping through the cracks.

Jake and I fall in line, waiting to get through security and into the lively chaos of the rodeo. I can hear the music from the arena and the distant whinnying of horses—it's... nostalgic. Bringing me back to the teenage days when Maisie was right here with me.

Just as those thoughts start to creep in, I do a double take toward the parking lot. It's like my mind conjured her out of nowhere, and suddenly, everything around me seems to pause. There she is—walking toward us, and it hits me hard, like a punch to the chest. She's rocking those knee-high boots and daisy dukes, but in a way that's so effortless, so her own. She's a little more laid-back than the other girls, but that only makes her more captivating.

It's enough to drive me wild. For a second, I swear gravity shifts, and I'm rooted to this spot, feeling this rush of heat flood through me. All those memories I've been trying to push down —the laughter, late-night talks, the way her eyes used to light up —surge up again. I can't shake them no matter how hard I try.

We're seventeen again, the last rodeo before senior year, and I see her walking up, laughing at something Olivia said. Her eyes scan the crowd, and then they land on me. That moment feels suspended—like time pauses—and her beautiful smile brightens even more. It's like I'm king again, the world narrowing down to just her and me in that instant.

I blink and it's gone, yet she's still smiling and walking toward us. Her sandy blonde hair catching the sunlight, parted half up with big, loose curls. She's always been stunning, but honestly, time has only made her more radiant. She's learned to embrace her natural beauty—without trying too hard. All thoughts of finding some "buckle bunny" instantly disappear, because there's no one I've ever seen who compares to her tonight.

She approaches us, waving at Jake with that genuine spark in her eyes. I'm frozen, completely in shock at what's transpiring between them. She leans down to chat with him.

"What's your favorite event to watch?" she asks him, but honestly, I'm so lost in her hazel eyes that I barely catch his response. My focus is all on how easy she makes it look, wrapping Jake in her laughter, mixing it with all the noise around us. She's effortlessly happy, and seeing her smile like that—especially at Jake? It's everything.

I'm barely even aware it's our turn to go through security, but Jake is ready. He steps up first, calmly goes through, and waits on the other side like it's no big deal. I wave Maisie forward, trying to memorize every detail of her face—like I might forget later. I think she says thanks, but it's quiet, and she quickly sets her phone and keys into the bin. She goes through, still joking with Jake, and I practically throw everything from my pockets into the tray. Coins fly everywhere, but all I can think about is how effortlessly happy she looks—teasing Jake, making jokes—like she's exactly where she's supposed to be. It crashes over me: this is everything I didn't realize I was missing. And instead of being cool and collected, I'm turning into a complete mess. My palms sweat, my chest races, and I'm pretty sure I look like a bumbling idiot.

The ticket line moves quickly, and just like that, we're on the other side. Maisie bends down to give Jake a quick hug, that big smile lighting up her face. "Have fun, guys!" she calls out, her voice bright and cheerful. But here's the kicker—she turns to leave, and for the first time in ages, our eyes meet. It's just a brief moment, but it feels like everything else fades away. Just me, her, and this heartbeat of a moment I wish could last forever. Then she breaks it, walking away like it didn't just rock my entire world. *What the fuck just happened?*

Thump, thump, thump. That's the sound of my heart, echoing in my ears as this mix of hope and confusion swells inside me. Sure, it wasn't exactly a conversation between us— did she even say anything directly to me? No. But the exchange with Jake feels huge somehow. *Why now? Is it because of Leo? Is she seeing him? Are they together now? Has she really moved on from being mad at me?*

My mom suddenly appears out of nowhere, loud and shouting for Jake. She's wearing a denim dress, a huge turquoise necklace, and the same vintage brown Stetson she's had since I swear I was Jake's age. Some might call it stylish; I'd say she's a little over the top—love her dearly, though.

Before I can even process what's happening, she's grabbed

Jake's hand and is dragging him away, completely oblivious to the catastrophic moment I just went through.

"I've got him!" she yells over her shoulder. "Have fun with your friends, Bubby!"

"Love ya, big guy! Be good for Gram!" Jake shoots me a thumbs-up before they melt into the crowd.

Questions swirl in my head like the dust kicked up from the arena as I make my way up the bleachers to find my friends. It takes me nearly twenty minutes to navigate the thick crowd, but I finally spot them near the top. Levi is sitting next to Odessa, and right beside her? *My Cowgirl Maisie.* The old nickname hits my brain so hard I nearly stumble, but I catch myself and keep going.

A quick glance at the crew they've assembled, and I let out a relieved breath that there's no sign of Leo or any of the other EFSC guys. Normally, I like having them around, they're easy to shoot-the-shit with, but I'm not sure my psyche can handle it right now.

Then, as if Maisie knew exactly what I was doing, the corner of her mouth tips up in an almost smile, and she gives me one small shake of her head. We used to do that back in the day, like we could read each others mind in a second. *What is happening? Two smiles in one day? How many heart attacks can a man have before he goes into cardiac arrest?*

I fight the urge to sit by her, and instead plop down beside Levi, striking up some chitchat with him and Odessa. Not even five minutes later, Luke comes storming up the bleachers, looking like he wants to rip Levi's head off. I've never seen Luke so jealous before, but with Odessa, it's like a switch flips. He always looks ready to handcuff anyone who stares at her for too long. They've only recently started dating, but the rumors have been flying for months.

I can't help but chuckle when Luke steps in front of me and

stands over Levi. He's built like a hockey player—broad shoulders, solid and imposing—while Levi, with his runner's build, is comparatively on the smaller side.

"Move, Turner." The tone in his voice is all kinds of possessive, and I'm grinning from ear to ear at seeing Luke so turned up.

"Excuse me," Levi says, clutching his chest like he's been mortally wounded. "Is there a problem, Sheriff?"

Luke smirks, arms crossed, looking like he's ready to mark his territory. "Yeah, my girl, my seat. Or your ass in handcuffs sitting in the back of my car."

"Oh, does he always talk this dirty?" Levi fires at Odessa who ends up cackling next to him.

"You have no idea…"

Levi may throw a little sass back at him, but he knows when to concede and moves down a row.

Then, without hesitation, Luke leans down and kisses Odessa, and suddenly, it's like everyone in the arena is watching them.

My phone buzzes aggressively in my pocket, pulling me away from the unfolding drama in the stands. I glance down, expecting my mom checking in, completely unaware of the spectacle right in front of me.

With a quick swipe, I answer, but my focus keeps drifting back to the crowd, still buzzing with excitement. Any moment now, I half-expect them to put Luke and Odessa on the kiss cam.

But my mom's voice crackles through the line, barely audible.

"What? Mom? I can't hear you!" I lean in, trying to block out the noise around me.

"Jake's missing!"

Panic shoots through me, and my heart skips a beat. "What

do you mean?!" I nearly shout, the words bursting out before I can stop them.

Her response is muffled, but a jolt of adrenaline kicks in, and I'm already on my feet, ready to sprint down the bleachers like I used to back in college. "Mom! Where are you?!"

Then Luke's hand clamps onto my shoulder, yanking me back hard. "Talk to me," he demands, his voice firm. I still try to shake off his grip instinctively, but when I finally meet his gaze, everything shifts.

The concern in his eyes stops me cold. It's the look of a devoted friend, someone who'd burn this rodeo down just to help me. "I have eyes and ears all over this place. Tell me what the hell is going on."

"Jake's missing." Just saying those two words feels like a weight dropping in my stomach, a chill creeping down my spine. The disbelief slams into me like a brick wall, and I struggle to catch my breath, my mind racing. *How could this be happening?*

Chapter Six

Maisie

The horror on Ethan's face when he demanded his mom tell him where Jake was felt like a knife to my gut. Suddenly, all those years of distance and turmoil vanished, and all I wanted to do was fix things. But how? How is Jake even missing? Winnie is so good with Jake—she always has her eye on him, careful and loving.

I heard Ethan shouting for answers over the noise of Odessa and Luke's grand kiss. He tried to stomp his way down, but Luke had him in a vice grip, spinning him around like he wasn't a six-foot-five, two-hundred-pound man. Then he unleashed that "I'm the sheriff in this town" voice. It's the same tone I swear he's had since he was barely a teen, but I don't think I've ever been close enough to feel the real authority behind it.

Ethan gives Luke a curt nod, agreeing to whatever Luke said, and just like that, his eyes find mine for the briefest moment. In that glance, I see everything—the fear, anger, and desperation of a parent who has just realized the worst has happened.

The two of them stampede down the metal bleachers, their footsteps loud against the chaos, and I can still hear Luke barking commands into his radio as they go.

My legs move on their own accord. I can't just sit here and wait—there has to be something, anything, I can do.

By the time I reach the bottom of the steps, the crowd is so thick that I have to dodge people just to keep up with the guys. *Where could my little Razz be? Maybe he's just lost? Or using one of the port-a-potties and hasn't come out yet?*

I shift direction, abandoning the way the guys were going, and head toward the far side where the nicest toilets are. There are two long rows, and since it's not near the beer stands, it's usually the cleanest option.

"Maybe we should think small? You know, like places a kid might hide for fun?" Odessa's voice cuts through my thoughts, and I glance over to see her easily keeping pace with me. Her long legs are at least twice the size of mine.

I nod, and we keep moving, our eyes scanning everything and everyone around us.

After we've checked every toilet in the vicinity, Odessa grabs my shoulders, forcing me to look at her.

'Okay, let's stop and think rationally for a second," Odessa suggests. Her hands remain planted firmly on me as she forces me to make eye contact.

"Odessa! We don't have time! What if—who knows what could have happened?!" The frustration bubbles up with every word as my heart races.

She takes a deep breath, her brow furrowing in concentration. "He's either hiding, sitting somewhere we don't know, or someone took him." Her tone is matter-of-fact, as if she's reading from a list in her head.

"Okay?" I reply, hoping to catch up to whatever she's thinking.

"Okay, so let's say worst-case scenario: someone ballsy enough came into a highly populated area and kidnapped him," her head shakes back and forth in disbelief. "Why? Who would do that? It can't be a coincidence that the golden boy of the NFL had his son taken."

"I don't—wait. Could it be Jake's mom?" I ask, my stomach twisting as the idea sinks in. No one really knows much about Ethan's baby mama—at least, no one's told me anything.

"Could be? Who is it?"

"How would I know? YOU were friends with him back then, not me!" I throw my hands up in exasperation, my voice rising slightly.

"Yeah, but I never saw him sleeping around!" She huffs out a breath, and then adds softer, "there were always girls lingering around, but he never looked twice."

"Not even when he was drunk?" I challenge.

"I only saw him drunk that one time!" It's like a lightbulb clicks on in her brain when she yells that, her eyes lighting up. "Oh my god. Stephanie!"

"Who?" I ask, confusion washing over me.

"The girl from the drive-thru! The one who drives the Jeep! It's her! I knew I recognized her! Oh my god. Oh my god. She was throwing herself at him that night." Her voice rises with each realization, and I can see the pieces falling into place in her mind.

"What Stephanie? What Jeep? What are you talking about?"

"Stephanie! The blonde chick from the day we went for the walk... Gorgeously overly filled blonde, the Jeep that's not like a Jeep Jeep, more like an SUV."

Her brain must be operating at a higher frequency than mine or something because I stand there staring at her, trying to make sense of who Stephanie is and what a not-Jeep Jeep is—

and then it hits me: a Jeep Cherokee or similar. My mind instantly rolls through every customer I have who drives a Jeep —Corey, Mrs. Ulma, The Marrio's, Hannah, Wren... The Marrio's! They don't live here full-time and use their house as a vacation rental. Which means...

"Stella?" I question trying to play catch up to how someone I thought was becoming a friend of mine is actually someone from Ethan's past. She fits all the boxes though—beautiful, blonde, driving the Marrio's Cherokee. *Of course, Ethan hooked up with the hottest woman I've ever seen in person—besides Odessa, that is.*

"Sure. But *that* night she was Stephanie, and was all over Ethan. I hadn't known they actually hooked up, but I'm not the least bit surprised she was always a punt bunny."

"Oh my god. She— That's—" The words catch in my throat, but it's all clicking into place. Her driving the Cherokee, but always describing her staying somewhere else. She was trying to throw me off her trail, and it totally worked.

I spin on the little heel of my boot and take off toward my car, which is still parked across town at Maisie's.

"Call Luke!" I shout over my shoulder as I sprint through the service exit. I make a mental note to scold Luke for allowing this exit to be open, but also say a little prayer to whomever upstairs is looking out for me.

Thank goodness, it's just us tearing through the lot with no one else around. Odessa keeps right up with me, her strides matching my frantic pace. I can practically feel it in my bones— Stella is really Stephanie.

The run to my car shouldn't take more than five minutes, but we get there way faster than I expected. My keys are already in my hand before I even realize it, but when I look down to hit the unlock button, I notice them quietly rattling due to my shaking. I toss them to Odessa, who catches them effortlessly, not even breaking a sweat. "You drive, I'll navigate."

Without missing a beat, she shoves the keys into the ignition and is reversing the car like someone is chasing us. For a brief moment, I just stare at her, truly appreciating the absolute ride-or-die personality that is Odessa Astor. For a supermodel, she is an actual badass.

"Back roads to out of town," I demand, snapping back to reality as the car rumbles beneath us.

"Okay—can you bullet point me on how you know where Stella's staying, the details on her being a customer, and whatever else might be pertinent info?" Odessa asks, steering through a corner faster than most would dare.

I take a deep breath. "She started coming in a few months ago... mid-April, maybe?"

"The 'Jeep' she's driving belongs to the Marrios—they own a vacation rental out at Jackie's Lake. Sometimes they let renters borrow their car. I *know* this because they've had that lake house forever. I used to help clean it with my mom, and the cars been parked in their garage for ages."

"Her first visit, I recognized the car right away, and she just kept talking about how beautiful it was here, waking up to the lake view. But then the next time—she completely switched it up and started talking about a view of the mountains instead."

"And, I mean," I pause, shaking my head slightly. "I thought it was weird since she was still driving their car, but honestly, I didn't think much of it. Maybe I figured she'd gone camping or something..."

"She was trying to cover her tracks, and it worked. Don't beat yourself up over it," Odessa says, shooting me an empathetic look as if she already knows where my head's at.

"I know, it's just—I can't help but wonder if 'Stella' was a slip because she almost said 'Stephanie'...?" It's tough trying to remember every conversation I've had with her, especially with how many customers I deal with each day. Still, I'm dissecting them all, hoping to catch something I missed.

"Turn right!" I shout, my voice rising as we nearly blow past the side road that leads us around the lake. The soft glow of twilight is fading fast, shadows creeping in and clawing at my nerves. We're only a few minutes away, but the tight ball of anxiety in my stomach feels like it's growing with each passing second.

"Okay, slow down. And, I don't know—turn off the lights?" I attempt to sound like I know what I'm doing, but I'm so out of my element, it isn't even funny. Action without planning isn't my forte, and that was a whole lot of action.

She does it, but meanwhile manages to drawl out, "We really should've called one of the guys."

"I did say to call Luke..."

"So that he can make us sit this one out? No. Plus, he's busy, and we are only doing recon, right?" *Right.*

We continue down the dimly lit road until the three cabins come into view. I point to the house at the top of the slight hill. I know the owners of all three—two are vacation rentals, but the other one belongs to my regulars, Louis and Cheryl Crownover. Thankfully, the cabin at the top belongs to the Crownovers, and I know they are also out of town.

Without thinking, I reached under my seat, grabbing my purse to pull out my Hellcat RDP. It's my go-to pistol at the range with Luke and the one I'm most comfortable using.

"Damn, girl. Who knew you were packing heat?"

I lean back and twist to flip open the center console, revealing the vault Luke helped me install. Inside, I keep my hot pink Ruger LCP—compact enough to fit in my car but still packing a serious punch. My finger glides along the digits, settling on the code Luke picked for me: 7-4-4-8.

"Another one? And it's PINK?!"

"Cousin's the sheriff."

"Oh, I know," Odessa replies, her tone dripping with innuendo. *Gross.*

Ignoring my look of disgust, she continues on. "I meant—it's just unexpected. You look so docile and... chippery."

"Chipper-y?" I glance down at my cut-off shorts adorned with embroidered daisies, my cowboy boots, and frilly top. *Okay, point taken.*

"Park in that driveway—it's the Crownover's, and they're in Spain right now."

From the top of Louis and Cheryl's driveway, we can see the cabin clearly. It looks mostly dark, with no porch or interior lights on. Once the sun goes completely down, it will be pitch black. A fresh wave of nerves skitters up my spine.

"Are you sure there's anyone in there?"

"Nope.."

"What's the layout? How many bedrooms and bathrooms?"

"This your first stakeout?" I question, turning to look at her through narrowed eyes.

She laughs once, "Pretending to be one of the Bod Squad right now and think how they would." *Good idea.*

"Three bedrooms. Primary is on the other side of the cabin and is huge, with its own walk-in bathroom. There's two bedrooms on this side, the one closest to the lake is the most accommodating and set up for renters. The smallest room is closest to us and is barely used.

"So, if she has him here, he'd be?"

"I don't know..." If she did take him, is it because she wants *him* or because she's using him to get something from Ethan?

"Worst-case scenario?" Odessa continues to prod. "Where would she keep him?"

"The primary bedroom has a walk-in closet. I don't remember if it locks, but there are no windows."

"Best-case scenario?" *He isn't there, and they already found him playing with a friend at the rodeo.*

"The second bedroom—I'd be able to see in and hopefully get him out."

Chapter Seven

Ethan

"Jake's missing." The words spiral frantically in my mind, panic clawing at my chest as I sprint towards the spot where my mom said she would be waiting. Behind me, I can hear Luke shouting into his radio, his urgency mirroring my own as he works to lock down the rodeo exits, stopping anyone from leaving or entering.

How could this happen? Jake's a good kid. He wouldn't just wander off or run away from my mom. Even as a toddler, he always stayed close, never more than an arm's reach away. The thought of someone taking him is a nightmare I refuse to believe—no way that happens here. Not in Three Sisters.

But this rodeo is huge—three-fourths of the crowd is made up of strangers. I push my way through the masses, scanning every face, searching for a glimpse of my mom or Jake. It's like looking for Waldo in the landscape of an old western movie. I want to tell myself that someone would've seen him leaving with some random person, but then my mind spirals again. What if the person wasn't random? The fear tightens in my chest, squeezing at my heart like a boa constrictor. *It couldn't be. She signed him away.*

Could that be what's happening? I fight to keep my head straight as panic swells, but every second feels like an eternity, and I just need to find them.

By the time I reach my mom, she is a mess—hysterical, drowning in her own fear and regret. She's on her knees in the dirt, dark bangs are matted to her face. Her red lipstick is smeared, mascara dripping down her face as Deputy Corbin crouches in front of her My dad is there, trying to soothe her, but it's like throwing water on a raging fire. She looks how I feel inside: frantic, helpless.

When I look at my dad, I see the disbelief on his face. He's nearly as tall as I am, and used to be built the same, but the years he's added a few more pounds.

"You need to talk to Deputy Ambrose, Winn," I hear him say, but she can't compose herself enough to form the words.

I rush to her side, crouching down to meet her tear-streaked face.

"Mom!" I plead, grabbing her shoulders. She throws her arms around me, and suddenly it's me who feels the weight of desperation. "You have to calm down. Please, tell us exactly what happened. We need to know so we can find him."

She heaves, her body vibrating as sobs break free. "We were... getting cotton candy, and the line was so long. I was talking to Elise and Cal. He asked if he could stand in the shade, just a bit off to the side—he wasn't more than ten feet away, I swear, Ethan. I swear!"

"I know, Mom. I know." The words feel inadequate against the weight of her anguish, but I believe every word she is saying.

"I kept looking over, and he was just hanging out there. Then... then he was just gone." Her voice cracks, panic and guilt flooding her face, twisting her features in a way that makes my heart ache even more.

"I called you immediately to see if he was with you. I didn't even wait a second." There's a desperation in her eyes, a flicker of helplessness that I'm sure reflects my own.

I can almost feel her guilt radiating off her, a dark cloud of self-blame hovering around her. I know my mom—she's always been hyper-aware of Jake, always keeping a watchful eye. And now, seeing her like this, I realize she's punishing herself far more than anyone else ever could.

"We'll find him." I reach out and put my hand on her shoulder, trying to ground us both amid the chaos swirling around us in a frenzy of shouts and worried faces.

Deputy Ambrose fires off more questions, but I can't focus. My eyes dart through the crowd, scanning every face—looking for whatever signs of Jake could be hiding in plain sight. Anyone who might have taken him.

Then Zeke shows up, the former chief of the Cascadia County sheriff's department and a family friend. His presence usually brings comfort, but right now it feels heavy.

"I already started protocol for a potential kidnapping," Luke informs him, and the word hits me like a punch to the gut.

Kidnapping. Hearing it out loud is like a physical blow. I've faced down three-hundred-pound men and felt less pain than I do now. *Jake. My Jake. Kidnapped.*

"Ethan." Zeke's hand lands on my shoulder, firm but steady. I glance over at him, and for a moment, I'm taken aback by how much he resembles his sons. But today, it's Dan I see— the solemn, serious, duty above all look that his departed son would have if he were still here.

"Could this be close to home?" he asks, and I instantly know what he's getting at. *Could it be Jake's bio mom?*

"I don't know." The words barely escape my lips, a whisper

caught in a swell of dread. My heart clenches as the reality sinks in; this isn't just about panic anymore—it's about something much darker.

My words are true, though, I have no idea. We didn't spend more than a night together when Jake was conceived, and I didn't see her again until she showed up at my penthouse, a week before her due date. I didn't want to believe her that he was mine, but I knew I'd hooked up with her that night. Knew I was drunk, knew I didn't bring my own protection. She offered her own, but I should've known better. We'd all heard the stories of the crazy women that poke holes in condoms or grab them from the trash bin. Should've known she was one of them.

Twenty-four hours later my phone rang, and the DNA test confirmed it. The baby growing in her belly, nearly at full term, was mine.

During that time I had my attorney draft the papers for her to give me sole rights and wire the money she said she needed for the "pain and suffering" of carrying my child to term. It was all legal—and I thought over. She said she never wanted to be a mom, never wanted the burden, but I guarantee she wanted the pay day. Little did she know, I'd have paid way more than half a million for Jake.

At least she told me before he was born. I was able to be there for his birth, name him, and they treated her as if she was nothing more than the surrogate. As soon as he was delivered we were escorted to another room—per her request, and I never saw her again. Never heard from her after that day.

That is until my phone gripped so tightly in my hand begins vibrating and when I see the screen it's three texts in succession.

UNKNOWN:

Jake's safe so long as you do what I ask.

Three million wired to an offshore account.

Veridian Bank, Port Blossom, Veridia, 132-4765-081293; 085764392

Chapter Eight

Maisie

"What's the plan?" Odessa asks as we both stare down the hill at the dark cabin. Isla once told me that the night she was attacked by Jeff felt like a scary movie; for the first time, I fully understand what she meant and just how terrifying that is. But am I going to do the smart thing and leave? Probably not.

The woods below are getting darker by the minute, every part of this feels ominous. But, she has Jake. I know it. Sweet, innocent Jake. Who wormed his little way into my heart, one raspberry Italian soda with extra whip at a time.

"You're going to stay here and keep trying to get service. Keep the doors locked. I'm only going to go look. He may not even be here—for all we know, they found him at the rodeo, and we are simply being creeps."

"Mais—" she starts to argue, but I cut her off and shake my head.

"Dess—I know this place like the back of my hand. I've been here so many times with my mom to clean after guests. I'll be fine, but I need you to wait here with the car on in case we need a quick getaway." I hand her the Ruger, and she takes it, pulling back the slide slightly and inspecting the chamber.

Reading my mind before I even ask, she says, "Brothers are SEALs." *Right, and the other flies helicopters into war-zones.*

I do a quick once over on my pistol, noting that the magazine is full.

Reaching into the back of my car, my fingers search the ground for the neoprene band that I wear while running. It conceals my gun perfectly under my shirt, and since I haven't confirmed that she's actually there, I don't want to go down there guns blazing.

Dear lord, please don't make me use this thing.

Once the pistol is secured, I reach for the handle and open the door, making sure not to look at Odessa. If I see the worry on her face, I'll surely chicken out.

The lights illuminate the car, and I quickly shut it so that we aren't seen. *If we haven't been already.*

I slowly make my way down the slope, stopping along some larger Pine tree's to catch my breath. I'm not moving quickly, but the adrenaline must be hitting hard because the only thing I can hear is my heavy breathing.

If I'm right about where she's keeping him, he'll be on the side of the house closest to us. Then again, maybe she's actually parenting him and I have it all wrong. It doesn't matter, I'm only here as a scout. I'm just going to see what's going on and then report back to Odessa. *Famous last words, Maisie.*

The lawn between the edges of the trees and the cabin isn't more than fifteen feet, a tiny sliver really, but it feels like a mile long without any cover.

The rough bark of the pine digs into my sweaty palms as I shove off it and sprint to the side of the house. My knees practically give as I go into a crouch and stay there—waiting, listening.

I don't hear anything but the hum of the A/C running. A good sign? Maybe. Someone is staying here at least.

I crouch walk toward the first window, the room that has two twin beds and is rarely used, and attempted to peek in, but it's completely dark in there.

Moving on, I make the same crouching walk to the next window. The room that has the queen-sized bed, but its own bathroom and TV.

This room is slightly illuminated, the small TV in the far corner on, but I can barely see anything.

The bed is to the side of the window, so close I have to switch to the other side of the window by ducking underneath. *God, what if it isn't Jake and I'm about to scare the hell out of some six-year-old tourist?*

I'm not tall by any means, but the base of the vertical window goes to chest level, and I can see perfectly in without standing on my tip toes.

The bed looks nearly made, except for a large lump on the side nearest the window.

Which means it's either Jake, or an excellent ruse and I'm about to have that horror movie moment.

Lightly, I tap on the window and watch the figure to see if it moves.

Nothing.

I tap a little harder and see the smallest shake begin to rock the bed. Goosebumps immediately spread across my skin as I stare at the blankets. *It has to be Jake. Please, please, dear lord, let it be him.*

"Jake," I whisper shout and tap twice again.

"Razz, it's me, Maisie." Using the nickname I gave him makes him lift a tiny bit of the corner of the blanket. I can barely make out the side of his face, but I see it's him, and tears spring in my eyes.

Before I can say anything else, he throws the blanket off him and scrambles out of bed toward the window.

He places his little hand on the other side and it's then I notice the handprint smears from where he clearly tried to get out already. If I wasn't doing my best to be strong for him, I'd have started sobbing right then.

He looks from me to the bottom of the window seal. The cabin has casement windows, which aren't exactly common anymore, especially not for a six-year-old that lives in the fanciest house in Three Sisters. The window has a crank that needs to be turned so that it can swing open or closed, depending on how much the person wants. *Currently, I want it off the freaking hinges.*

I point toward the lock and make a pinching motion, "pull it out" I mouth.

He copies my movement like a little champ, his body still shaking, but his eyes light up when it comes out a few inches. I nod my encouragement, even though all I want to do is cry still.

I use my hand to motion how he should turn the handle while going the opposite way so that it's mirrored for him.

The window starts to push out and as soon as my fingers can get through the crack, I rip it the rest of the way, breaking the hinge that's meant to only let it go a few inches.

Before I can reach for Jake, something hard is jammed into my back.

Oh, fudge.

Chapter Nine

Ethan

My knee bounces a million miles a minute as I sit in Luke's office, the turmoil outside deafening. He won't let me leave, won't even hand over my phone—probably knows I'd do something reckless, like send her my entire bank account.

One hour, thirty minutes.

It hasn't even been two hours since I got that call, but it feels like a lifetime. I know an Amber Alert's gone out. I know every single resident of Three Sisters is looking for Jake by now. I know Hayes has already assembled his team, and every guy I didn't want to see a few hours ago is now pouring their heart into finding him. I know that the people I trust most in the world are searching, and yet... it's not enough.

Luke paces outside the door, barking out orders, taking calls —never stopping, never hesitating. Since I learned Jake was gone, he's been relentless, as if all his training and leadership have been embedded into that single moment. His fierce determination is the only thing holding me in this chair, because I know, without a doubt, he'll do everything he can to bring Jake back to me.

My mom was here, probably still is—somewhere—nearly inconsolable, blaming herself. I should've told her I know it's not her fault, that Stephanie was always manipulative and a bitch. I should've prepared for this moment. Should've known what she was capable of and prevented it.

But I didn't. I didn't do anything except stand there in that same spot, watching everyone at the rodeo stop what they were doing to search for Jake.

When it became clear he wasn't there—and she already had him— Luke ordered us to regroup at the station.

Now I sit in quiet helplessness, staring at Luke's desk while he handles the most terrifying moment of my entire life.

And giving up control? There's nothing more humbling. Nothing more devastating.

Chapter Ten

Maisie

"Really, Maisie?" I recognized Stella's, Stephanie's, voice right away. And let me tell you, it's a lot more obnoxious sounding now that I know what a total brat she is.

Jake's eyes go wide, and he instinctively steps back from the window. *Don't worry, Raspberry.* Luke's been annoying me with this simulation for years.

Pay attention, watch for mistakes, surprise hits.

The first thing I notice is that whatever initially hit my back isn't pushed in as hard anymore. *Sloppy.*

Calmly, I slowly twist around, my palms open and in mock surrender until I'm face to face with the blonde I thought I was friends with, a gun to my chest. Ironically, pointed at the gun that is concealed under my shirt.

The sneer on her face sends rage pulsing through my body. I don't curse often, but in this case, I may break my rule and say something mama wouldn't approve of. *And up close, really not all that pretty.*

"Why am I not surprised you're—?" I step to the side of her

so fast, she doesn't even blink. My left-hand races out and latches onto the barrel of the gun, at the same time my right hand comes around to the back of the gun and pulls down. She was holding it so loosely it practically falls out of her hand, and she stumbles in shock, a gasp of pain from where her fingers were stuck.

Before I can aim her gun at her, she launches herself at me.

She's like a cat trying to claw its prey's eyes out—all sharp talons and hissing. Her gun goes flying in the direction of the woods, but luckily I can still feel that mine is in place. The problem is that while she's only nails and untrained hits, she's wild and thrashing so much that I don't want to reach for my gun.

An open slap lands hard across the side of my head and a tingling sensation rolls through my skull—*Ok-aaay. Not cool.*— Somehow, I manage to get my hands on her chest and shove her as hard as I can, and she stumbles back.

The stinging on my face doesn't let up, but I know I need to refocus and set a plan—only she's coming at me again before I can move.

Alright—Hand-to-hand combat. Luke would approve.

Trying to get myself into a better position, I drop my left leg back and pull my hands up level with my head. She doesn't even notice I'm getting into a striking position as she reaches for my hair, nearly grabbing a fistful. Before she can, my fist flies at the side of her head and by the pain radiating from my hand to my elbow, it's a solid hit.

She folds backward, her body going completely still on the ground, and for once, I'm thankful for the years of "surprise attacks" from Luke. The gun that flew out of my hands is still in the grass, and I sprint for it, yanking it off the cold ground before turning back toward Jake.

Stephanie is still sprawled in the grass, as if she was

about to make a snow angel, but is now perfectly still. I pass by her, only glancing down to make sure she really is knocked out.

"Maisie!" Little arms are wrapped around my neck as I pull him the rest of the way through the window.

"You're okay, Razzy," I assert, as he wraps his legs around me, and I pull his head to my shoulder. His tiny body shivers against me, but I start running the same way I came, quickly putting distance between us.

It may have been a darn good knockout, but I don't trust that she's alone in this. Shoot, that thought alone has me pushing myself harder up the hill.

As soon as I get to my car, I throw open the back door and Odessa screams.

"DRIVE" I shout back, diving into the back seat. Thankfully, Jake has practically suction cupped himself to my front, so he moves with me like we are one.

Without hesitation, she hits the gas, the momentum slamming the door shut behind us.

"Razz, you're okay, but we have to buckle you. Okay?" He doesn't even lift his head from my shoulder, only squeezes tighter.

"Jake, I promise Dess is gonna drive us straight to your daddy, but we've gotta get you there in one piece," I say, trying to pry him off me. "I'll hold you the whole way, but we both need our seatbelts."

He slowly peels his head off my shoulder, and I see tears streaming down his face. "I don't... have... my... booster seat!" he wails, throwing his head onto my shoulder again and squeezing me even tighter.

I make eye contact with Odessa, the same thought passing between us—rage for Stephanie and sadness for Jake.

"Listen, I promise this will be the last car ride you go on

without one, but seatbelts are safer than nothing. Sit in the middle, next to me. I'll hold you the whole time, I swear."

Finally, he relents and moves to the side. I buckle him first in the middle seat, and then buckle myself. I'm not sure who taught Odessa to drive like she's in the Indie 500, but I remind myself to bake them something extra special and give them free coffees for life—Her, as well, for being my partner in crime.

We hit speeds I didn't know my car could do, but never once do I feel unsafe. She pushes it, but not so much that I'm ever worried about our safety. Or maybe my threshold for stress after just having a gun pointed at my head is higher.

Not until headlights appear behind us, that is.

They fly up so fast that the only reason I notice them is because of the small intake of breath Odessa does. We are maybe twenty minutes from town, but we still haven't hit the main road.

"Just keep driving, Dess."

She nods and from the back I see how white her knuckles are. I pull my phone out, praying there's service but nothing goes through when I dial 911.

That doesn't stop me from trying, though. I call and call and call. Until at last, I hear the ringing tone. Like the car behind knows, it backs off. Stopping all together.

"911, what's your emergency?"

"It's Maisie Jones—I have Jake! Tell Luke and have him get to Ethan! I have Jake." The last part is nearly choked out of me.

"Maisie?" I recognize Paige's voice as it gasps. There aren't too many dispatchers at the Cascadia County Sheriff's Office, and she's one of my regulars.

"Paige! Call Luke! We are almost to Highway 20 from Jackie's Lake. He was at the Marrio's cabin. Stella—Stephanie —took him."

"All units, the Amber Alert has been canceled. Missing child has been found..."

Jake's grip on my arm tightens, and I squeeze his knee back.

He's okay.

I found him.

He's safe...

And, I didn't freeze.

Chapter Eleven

Ethan

"Where are they?" Luke demands, stomping toward his office like he's ready to tear through the place for answers. I'm on my feet in a split second, my heart sinking somewhere deep in my gut. *Please let him be okay.*

His eyes meet mine, a moment of raw intensity passes between us, and I can see the truth—Jake is safe. Relief and urgency swirl in his expression. He still has a job to do, but it's clear that Jake is okay.

"Who found him?" Luke asks into his radio, but his focus is still on me. Then I see it: shock washes over his face, his mouth actually drops open as he inhales instantaneously. A look I've never seen before on him, that nearly sends a chill down my spine. He's seen everything, and whoever found Jake must be someone he never expected.

"Who?" I croak, my throat dry.

Luke hesitates, and we lock eyes, a silent contest of who can hold the gaze the longest.

He gives in first, sighing and mouthing, "Maisie." Hearing that is the moment my knees decided to buckle. I dropped to the floor like all the strength in me was yanked away. *Maisie found him? Maisie saved him? How? Why?*

Luke starts barking orders, but his words become a muddled blur in my ears. I'm fixated on the fact that Maisie is the one who rescued my son. Where did she find him?

Still on my knees, I watch Luke, but it's like he's speaking a foreign language—everything is moving so fast. It isn't until he stands in front of me again, pulling me back up, that I snap back to reality.

"Jake's okay. He's safe, no visible harm or injuries. Maisie found him at the Marrio's cabin. I don't know much else, but I sent deputies out there to see if Stephanie's still there. By the time the girls got service, it'd have given her at least a twenty-minute head start, though." *The girls?*

"Maisie and Odessa." He must see the confusion on my face because he adds it without me having to ask.

He squeezes my arm, urging me forward. "Come on, they're going to the back." He hands me my phone back, but I don't even look at it, only pocket it to deal with at another time.

I follow behind him like a duckling following its mom. I'm on autopilot. I should feel relieved; I should be elated, but all I feel is anxiety. I need to see him. I need to hold him. Both of them. Shit, add Odessa into that mix too. That woman is a true friend, willing to do whatever she can for her people.

As we move through the brightly lit hallway, I glance at the black-and-white candid photos of deputies at various town events. I recognize every face, and it's not lost on me that at least three-fourths of them helped tonight to find Jake. Three Sisters isn't just a community; it's a family. One I owe a hell of a lot to after witnessing firsthand the lengths they'd go to—shutting down the town for me.

The employee parking lot is bathed in light, but beyond the gates, shadows creep in. Every time a car passes by, I hold my breath, exhaling only when it continues down the road. But when the red and blue lights flash down the street, I know it's them. Maisie's car pulls in slowly behind a deputy cruiser, and just the sight of it has my heart rate spiking.

The cruiser rolls past, and I don't even bother glancing at it. I focus instead on the front seat, catching a glimpse of Odessa's ash-blonde hair, but it's the sight of Maisie behind her that snaps my attention. Her long wavy locks frame her face as she cradles my son in her arms. My, tall for his age, son, looks to be about her size right now. Even though I know he's much smaller.

In a rush, I throw myself forward, pulling on the back door handle, but it doesn't budge—still locked from the drive here. Frustration bubbles up inside me, and suddenly, I'm the impatient kid yanking on the handle over and over again.

Out of the corner of my eye, I see Odessa flustered, fumbling to unlock the door. Finally, I hear the click, and the door swings open with my pull. Instead of letting them out, I slide in myself, pulling them both into a bone-crushing embrace.

Maisie tries to pull away, but Jake's arms are locked tight around her, and mine are snug around both of them. Her light giggle pierces through my tension, lifting the burden just a little. It's a sound I've missed, one that feels just as familiar as it once was. Tears blur my vision as the overwhelming emotion hits hard. *She fucking saved him. How?*

"Look, Razzy. Dad's here." Something in the way she says 'dad' hits me.

"Dad!" Jake cries, letting go of Maisie just enough for me to get a good look at his tear-streaked face.

I pull him in close, wrapping him up as best I can around the seatbelt. "You're okay, big guy. You're okay." My heart swells with relief as I feel him relax. "Maisie found you, huh?"

"She saved me, Dad! She did this ninja move to get the gun and then beat up that crazy lady!"

"What?!" I shout at Maisie, the surprise echoing in my voice. She just shrinks back a little, her cheeks flushing.

"Yeah, well, yeah," she says with a casual shrug that makes my disbelief clash with the truth of her words.

"Always, My Fierce Maisie," I reply, the nickname tumbling out like a long-lost echo, raspy from disuse. Something about the way she flinches at it, a flicker across her face, makes me wonder if I crossed a line or if there's something I'm missing.

Odessa's head pokes in from the front seat, pulling my attention. I hadn't even noticed she'd gotten out, but I'm sure Luke had something to do with that.

"You three ready to go inside? Maybe get Jake some hot chocolate or something?"

A breath of relief escapes me as Jake nods eagerly, "Yes!" he shouts, pumping his little fist. Kids are something else—kidnapped, rescued, and still hyped for hot chocolate.

Maisie turns first and opens the door, Jake following close behind her and then me. I notice a few deputies standing around; the same relief on their faces.

Jake clings to Maisie's hand, as well as mine, we head back into the department. Luke leads us into the break room, chatting animatedly with Jake to keep things feeling normal, cracking jokes about the offices we pass. It's working; I see a few of those funny, carefree laughs from my boy.

"Coffee or hot cocoa, Mais?" Luke asks, glancing between us.

"Both? I want sugar and caffeine in the same cup!" she jokes, and I can't help but chuckle.

Luke glances my way, and I nod my agreement. "Same here. I want my creamer in the form of hot chocolate."

"Want me to help? I am the expert here," Maisie says, but Jake's eyes go wide as he clutches her hand tighter, as if letting go would mean losing her.

"Don't go!"

"Oh!" Maisie looks down at Jake, surprise flashing across her face at his outburst. Then her expression softens, radiating warmth and kindness. "I think you're right, Raspberry. We've done enough hard work tonight. Let's sit back, and let Luke make us something yummy. Is that okay?"

He nods eagerly, eyes wide. "Do you have any whip, Uncle Luke?"

Luke grins mischievously. "You know, I, personally, do not. But if memory serves, Jill brought some in the other day for a pie she made, and I think she'd be happy to share with us."

"How about we sit on the couches and wait?" Maisie bends down to Jake's level, and I can't help but marvel at the interaction. *How is she so good with him? Why does it feel like everything I've ever wanted and more?*

We follow her, Jake's hand still in hers and mine holding on to his other small hand.

The loveseat isn't big, but she perches on the edge, leaving as much space for Jake and me as she can. I try to sit so it looks like Jake barely fits between us, which forces me to throw my arm around the back of him. Then I set my hand on her shoulder and gently pull her back, encouraging her to relax. Maisie gives me an inch, and I'll take a mile—always have, always will.

And the best part? She lets me. Her body relaxes as she leans back, and together, the three of us settle comfortably on this cozy little couch.

Odessa is across from us on the other loveseat, her eyes darting from Luke making our drinks, back to us. When they meet mine, she offers a small sympathetic smile.

"Thank you," I mouth, and she nods quickly before looking away.

I sense Maisie's eyes flitting between us, and when I glance over, I catch a flicker of jealousy in her gaze. *Interesting.*

I squeeze her shoulder lightly until she looks at me, really looks at me, and then I shake my head, mimicking the way she had earlier at the rodeo.

A silent conversation passes between us, her eyes locked on mine, as if she's trying to read my mind. And then she smiles, the smallest tip of the corner of her mouth, but it's pure relief on her part. One small smile, and just like that, twelve years later, there's hope again.

Luke strides back in with three mugs, handing them to the girls and Jake first before heading back for ours.

"Your mom is on her way. Zeke went to your parents' house to let them know, and she insisted on it."

"Grandma?" Jake asks, looking up at me with those wide, innocent eyes.

I nod, and I can see the worry start to creep onto his face. "She was probably so worried. That lady said you were hurt, and that I needed to go right to you. I told her we should tell Grandma, but she said Grandma would want me to go."

"It's okay, big guy..." I maintain a calm voice, despite internally screaming.

"She tricked me, though. Right?"

"Yeah, yeah, she did," I admit.

"Do you think you can tell us what happened after that, Jake?" Luke asks, his tone casual—like he's just "Uncle Luke" rather than the sheriff investigating a crime.

Jake shrugs. "Not much. We ran past the nice potties and to a car."

"I knew it!" Maisie exclaims, full of excitement. We all turn to look at her. "Sorry. I just—that's the exit we left out of, too. There wasn't any security near it."

Luke furrows his brow. "I'll look into that."

"Go on, Jake," he encourages.

"We got into this car, and I didn't even have my seat," Jake says, frowning. I feel Maisie freeze, and when we make eye contact, I see rage flicker in her eyes—like she's ready to explode. Jake continues, "I told her I always ride in a booster, and she said it was an emergency and it didn't matter." *Dumb bitch.*

I huff out a breath before I can stop myself, and Jake glances up at me. "I'm sorry, Daddy."

"No. It's not your fault. She did a bad thing; not you," I say, trying to keep my voice steady.

Maisie nods, patting the hand she's still holding. "Dad's right. Adults get tricked all the time by bad people. Ask Luke—he sees it all the time."

Luke gives a serious nod when Jake looks at him. "Way too much. People can say some pretty crazy things to get what they want. What happened after you got in the car?"

"I don't know. It felt like she drove forever, and she got mad any time I asked a question." My insides twist as I tense at every word he says, and I have to consciously remind myself to stay calm. Jake needs me strong. "There was a lake I saw out the window, and then she parked in this garage thing that wasn't attached to the house. Then she put me in a room with cartoons and told me not to leave or move. I tried to get out the window, but I couldn't make it open..." The weight of his sadness hits me hard, and judging by the look on everyone else in the rooms faces, I'd say they're feeling the same.

"Wow. You were very brave to do that," I say, trying to keep my voice steady.

Just then, my phone pings twice, pulling my attention. I catch Luke's eye as he raises an eyebrow.

UNKNOWN:

Game on, Ethan.

Until I see that money in my account—or something just as good as three mil—your girl better watch her back.

Fuck.

Chapter Twelve

Maisie

The two dings from Ethan's phone send us all casting side-eyes his way. It's like we've been collectively holding our breath, just waiting for Stephanie to reach out. And somehow, we all know it's her. Then I watch the color drain from his face, shoulders tense up, and the hand that was cruising for comfort on my shoulder starts to shake.

He rolls his neck like he's trying to shake off the tension before looking over at Jake. "Hey, big guy, I need to chat with Uncle Luke about something. You cool to hang with Maisie for a sec? I'll be right back." He points through the glass window toward the hall.

Jake gives a nod, snuggling in closer to me.

"I've got him." I shoot Ethan a reassuring smile, but the way he looks at me makes me want to crawl out of my skin. Ethan Flacco is still just as hot as he was when I was sixteen, and that undivided attention? Still enough to wreck me for a lifetime.

Luke follows Ethan into the hall, and I try not to eavesdrop, but how can I not? He looks all kinds of tense, like a volcano about to blow, as he hands his phone to Luke.

Luke reads the message, his expression changing as he pulls out his phone, making whatever calls he needs to.

I steal a glance at Odessa; worry lines her face. Thankfully, Jake seems oblivious to the tension, sipping his hot chocolate with his head resting on my arm. I'm sure mine is equally as good, but the sudden churning in my stomach has me resisting a drink.

When both guys stroll back in, I can immediately tell that whatever was on Ethan's phone wasn't good. They both look like they want to roll heads, but they're forced to keep a normal appearance for Jake's sake.

Luke shoots me that sympathetic look he always used—whenever a townie would bring Ethan up—like he's saying, "I'll kick their butt if you want me to, but you brought this on yourself."

"You did good, Jake. You stayed calm and were so brave until Maisie and Odessa found you. Speaking of which, how did you find him?" Luke turns in his seat, focusing on Odessa, who sits next to him. *Oh, fiddle-sticks. Here we go.*

I know that look too—it's two parts 'what the heck were you thinking,' and one part 'I'm so livid you put yourself in danger I can't think straight.'

For a moment, Odessa's mouth falls open, as if she wasn't prepared for him to question her. Then, she tips her chin so far up that it could only be described as her attempting to look down her nose at him. *You go, girl!*

"We were following a hunch," she admits, albeit defiantly. "After we found out Jake was missing, Maisie and I started brainstorming. A few weeks back, she had a customer who looked familiar to me, but I couldn't quite place where I knew her from. That is, until I remembered..." Her gaze flicks to Ethan, one arched brow raised in question.

Ethan's face is like stone, but he gives the slightest nod.

"I told Maisie, and apparently, the woman had become a regular. Maisie recognized the Jeep she drove as being The... Marrio's?"

"And you didn't think to loop us in—not even one of the countless deputies hanging around?" Luke's voice is low, and I can feel the storm brewing behind his eyes.

"It was just a hunch!" I nearly shout, but Odessa has her moment too, turning to Luke and saying, "Save the lecture for later, Sheriff."

Luke's eyes darken, flicking between us; his stance mirroring Ethan's. They're both clearly annoyed we ran off without telling them, but frankly? I couldn't care less. Jake's safe, and that's what matters most.

The tension vanishes instantly when Ethan's parents, Winnie and Bruce, burst through the door. Winnie nearly trips over her feet the moment she spots Jake, but Bruce is quick to steady her. She looks like a completely devastated mess—eyes puffy and cheeks stained red from crying.

Jake bolts over and wraps his arms around her. "I'm sorry, Grammy!"

Tears streak down her face as she gently comforts him, "It's okay, sweetheart." Just then, Olivia and Drew seem to materialize out of nowhere, like they've appeared from thin air. She quickly ducks around them to reach Ethan.

Drew, nearly the same height and build as Luke, stands beside Odessa—darker hair, sharper features, with an edge that makes him look more polished than country. He gives both of us a contemplative look, his gaze steady. I catch his quiet sarcastic remark, "What, you quit modeling to start a P.I. business?"

Luke just grunts, moving to shake Drew's hand, trying to keep things serious, but the tension's thick enough to cut.

Olivia's pretty quiet as she hugs Ethan; her big eight-month belly hidden behind him. I stand awkwardly to the side, feeling out of place. The three of us used to be so close—Ethan, Olivia, and me—and now it feels like they're a unit, and I'm on the outside looking in. That familiar pang hits me again, echoing every time I see them together. I've always been thankful they stayed close, and that Ethan still has her friendship, but jealousy is a wicked beast. Especially when a part of me still aches from what tore us apart, making me realize how much I lost—and how much I still wish I could have been a part of it all.

When Olivia finally pulls away from Ethan, she turns and hugs me, tears and snot running down her face. "Mais—are you okay?" she whispers just for me to hear.

The way she asks makes me wonder if she's concerned about my run-in with Stephanie, about being around Ethan so much, or if she senses that everything is about to change.

What do I even say? Because sure, finding Jake and everything that came with that will take time to unpack. But genuinely, it's this moment—this intense, pressing moment—that's crashing down on me, and I can't help but freak out. I've spent years avoiding Ethan, building this wall to keep him at a distance. I'd hoped that one day I might let go of my feelings—and that we could share some small talk. But now, here I am, standing on the edge, fully aware that he's back in my life.

As much as I try to resist, my eyes are drawn to him, wrapped in his mom's embrace. Our gazes lock, and there's this raw emotion in his eyes—the kind of look that screams he just thought he lost everything, and I'm the one who helped bring it back to him.

"I'm so screwed," I murmur back to Olivia, the weight of it all sinking in.

A hand lands on my shoulder, and I turn to see Drew grinning at me. "I'd offer you a job if you didn't make the best chocolate chip cookies in town." Heat rushes to my cheeks.

Considering he only hires former special forces, I highly doubt that, but I appreciate his attempt to lighten the mood with some good-hearted humor.

"Drew! You should've seen her knock the gun out of that lady's hand!" Jake shouts from across the room, and I wince as all eyes turn to me.

"Luke taught me a few things when I first opened the hut," I divulge, trying to downplay it.

Luke mutters a curse under his breath, his expression tight, while Ethan's back goes ramrod straight. But Drew just beams at me, clearly impressed.

"*Badass*, Maisie. You and Charlie should totally start a Women's Self-Defense class in town!"

I can feel my face turning into a cherry tomato, but before I can respond, Winnie rushes over and wraps me in a hug. "You'll come over tomorrow and tell me everything that happened, right?"

Luke lets out an exaggerated sigh, "It's getting late. We should all head home. Mais, I need you to stay at my place—"

"Why?"

He shoots me a look that says, "we'll talk later," but before I can press him, Jake comes running over.

"No! Stay with us, please! I'll be scared without you."

"Razz—" I glance at Ethan, who's visibly fighting a grin, his lips twitching.

"You heard him, Mais. He'll be scared without you." Just like that, it's as if a decade melts away. And the way he's looking at me, like I'm Jake's only hope, makes it impossible to say no.

"Okay." *I am so, so screwed.*

Chapter Thirteen

Maisie

"You'll ride with us, right?" Jake asks, latching onto my hand once again.

I feel a wave of exhaustion wash over me—I'm overwhelmed and a bit terrified. Sure, I could insist on driving my car, but what would that achieve besides proving my stubbornness? I doubt I'd even make it there without turning back, which would only disappoint Jake.

So, for once, I take the easy route and give in without a fight.

Ethan jogs ahead and opens the rear door of his truck—the same one he's been driving since he came back—and I can't shake the feeling that tonight is a full circle moment.

He reaches down to lift Jake, but as I attempt to release my grip, Jake holds on tighter. When Ethan swings him up, I stumble forward, falling into Ethans back.

With one hand still clutching Jake, I'm forced to brace myself against Ethan, my palm pressing against the hard planes of his stomach. *Darn you and your still-perfect body, Ethan Flacco!*

Given how his body tenses beneath me, I'd say he's feeling it too. And then he has the audacity to laugh.

"Sorry," I murmur, trying to pull away before I do something stupid—like lean in and breathe in the scent of his shirt. My hand slips away easily, but as I struggle to free Jake's death grip, I hear his soft plea.

"Maisie... Could you—can you? Sit by me?" Jake's nervous voice makes both our shoulders tense up. He might've seemed braver back in the break room, but I can't blame him for needing comfort now. Ethan turns to look over his shoulder at me, raising an eyebrow as if to see if I sense the shift too.

My heart squeezes as it tries to grasp the weight of Jake's vulnerability, and I have to swallow the lump in my throat before I can respond. I try to keep it cheerful: "Wouldn't want to sit anywhere else, Razzy."

Ethan finishes buckling him in and leans forward to plant a gentle kiss on Jake's forehead. Then he turns to face me, and like a moth to a flame, I can't look away. Ethan's hand brushes lightly down the side of my face as he whispers, "Thank you."

And just like that, he twists away, moving quietly to stand behind me, his hand resting on the door while he waits for me to climb in.

I carefully make my way around Jake and his booster seat, determined not to let go of the hand he's still gripping until I'm seated and can switch hands.

The drive's short, but every bump feels like a mile as we pass my parents' driveway. I haven't gone past it since the day he caught me on my run and told me "they" were building on it. Had I known at the time there wasn't another woman, would it have changed anything? Probably not. But it may have hurt a little less.

Riding past the spot where he broke the news hits me hard. The dream house. My dream house. Overlooking the ranch where I grew up, the same hill where we'd sit together, dreaming aloud about our futures—him making it in the NFL, and me owning a bakery and starting a family, crafting the life I always wanted. Now it's his house. His and Jake's. While I'm thrilled Jake gets that life, I can't shake the feeling that he took my dream and made it his reality. So why on earth did I ever agree to a sleepover?

"I really shouldn't—" I start to say as Ethan hits the keypad to unlock the gate.

"Nope," he interrupts, turning to look at me. "Jake insisted, and he's had a shitty day. Please, just do this for him." *Ugh.* It's as though he knows the Jake card will always work. And as I glance down at the sleeping Jake, his head resting on my shoulder, I realize how true that is.

"And there are some things we need to talk about." *Nope. Nope. Nope. We are so not going there!*

"Ethan—"

"About Stephanie—there's more. Some texts. Just please." The desperation in his voice tugs at me, and against my better judgment, I nod. I push aside the flutter in my stomach as we coast through the gate and up the winding hill.

As we round a corner, my breath catches. It's the exact house I once described to him, my fantasies crashing into reality. Everything's lit up by outdoor lights, really showing off the grandeur of not only the house but also the stunning landscaping surrounding it.

I can only sit there, speechless, my eyes glued to the farmhouse-style house in front of me. The decorative railings and latticework along the wraparound porch, rocking chairs that look like they came straight out of my daydreams, and those high dormer windows give it this charm—like it should be in the South instead of Central Oregon.

"How do you keep it so white?" I finally manage to whisper

as a wave of nostalgia washes over me. He would tease me mercilessly about how impractical white was—it'd turn tan before the paint even dried.

He chuckles lightly, "I have a guy who comes out."

"It's... beautiful." I dare a glance at him, wishing I knew what he was thinking as he gazes at the house. He doesn't say anything for what feels like forever, just staring at it as if he's soaking in every detail.

Then he softly says, "Yeah, it really is. But I can't take the credit for it. Someone once told me in detail what the perfect house would look like, and I only replicated it." His words linger heavily in the air, stirring a mix of memories and something deeper inside me.

"You stole my dream?" I try to joke, hoping to lighten the mood, but my voice comes out raspy.

"No, I made it come true," he replies. I inhale sharply at his words, the way he says it as if he's finally confessing—like this house was always meant for me.

When I turn to look at him, he's not focused on the house anymore—his eyes are locked on me. The intensity in his gaze feels electric, and I can't look away. Yet, I feel the anxiety starting to swirl low in my gut, whispering that I'm not ready for this.

Then, gratefully, a sleepy voice breaks the moment: "Are we home?"

My gaze snaps away so fast you'd think we'd been caught doing something we shouldn't have.

"Yeah, big guy," Ethan says with a light and cheerful tone that feels almost surreal after our earlier stare-down. "I was thinking, sleepover in my room?" *Whaaaat? No!*

"Yes!" Jake pumps his fist in the air, excitement radiating off him. "You'll love it! Dad's bed is huge!"

Before I can even protest, Ethan opens his door and climbs

out. Jake clicks the button on his seatbelt and gives me a look that clearly says, "Let's go."

My door swings open next, and there's Ethan, flashing that devilish smile that used to always make my heart flutter. "Need help, My Sleepy Maisie?"

"Why'd you call her that?" Jake asks, laughter bubbling up like it's the most natural thing in the world.

"It's our thing." And the way he shrugs so casually makes me realize just how much I've missed the closeness we shared. "The middle word changes, but she's always been mine." *Oh, fuu—dge.*

"Oh! We have a thing too... she calls me Razzy!" Jake chimes in, clearly proud of his nickname.

"I thought I heard that. What's up with that?" Ethan asks, glancing back and forth between us, his brows furrowing confused.

"Raspberry's my favorite, Dad," Jake replies matter-of-factly.

Ethan nods, knowingly. "Yeah, but how does she know that?"

"Because Grammy takes me to see Maisie on our Fridays! But we aren't supposed to tell you because it might make you sad that you don't get to have any."

"Wait! I thought you knew!" I blurt out, my cheeks heating up.

"Since when?!" He fixes me with that intense gaze.

"Uhm," I stammer, scrambling for the right words. Memories flood back—Winnie just showing up like it was no big deal, the windows rolled down and Jake grinning from ear to ear in his carseat. "I think she started bringing him when he was just over a year old? He had chocolate milk back then, but then he switched to raspberry Italian sodas."

"Almost five years," Jake chimes in proudly, clearly pleased with his math skills, and I can't help but cringe a little.

Ethan's gaze bounces between us, clearly unsure how to react, and then he lets out an exaggerated huff. "You," he says, pointing at me, "owe me five years of coffees, pastries, cookies— all of it. I'm not having it smuggled to me anymore!" I knew he was getting them brought to him, but I could never prove it. Just like I'm sure he knows I have Margie bring me her leftovers whenever they go to Ponderosa Pine.

Amused, I can't help but laugh a little. "I literally just saved your kid, but *okay.*"

Suddenly, Ethan's right in front of me, grabbing my chin in his hand and tilting my face up to his. For a heartbeat, I forget Jake's even there, overwhelmed by the feeling that he's about to kiss me. *Do I want that?*

Before I can decide, he says, "You're right. I'll never be able to repay you for that."

"Can we watch a movie tonight?" Jake asks, totally breaking the spell.

Ethan relaxes a bit, releasing me. "Maybe a quick show. Come on, let's show Mais the house."

Just like that, the moment shifts. We're no longer lost in that charged space between us. Instead, there's a rush of excitement as Jake drags me along, eager to explore the home I've dreamed about but never thought I'd see up close.

And let me tell you, it's everything I imagined. Inside and out. It's as if Ethan took notes on all the things I said and made sure it was perfect. Five bedrooms, a home gym, bathrooms I lost count of, and a kitchen that opens up to a cozy nook over-looking the fields. A basement that has a game room, movie theater, and kids obstacle course. The house is designed to highlight the view, setback from the edge of the hill more than I expected, making space for the large backyard and patio.

Jake chatters excitedly throughout the tour, showing me all his favorite spots, and by the time we reach his room, I'm completely worn out.

"Isn't it so cool? Dad let me pick out all the stuff for my last birthday, so I could have a big kid room." The entire room is baseball-themed—memorabilia on the walls, shelves filled with baseball cards, and posters of his favorite players. There's a baseball net in the corner where he can practice swings, and a bed shaped like a baseball glove, complete with stitching details. Even the curtains have tiny baseballs embroidered on them.

I glance at Ethan, my eyes asking the unspoken question— he's the all-time great football player, after all. He just rolls his eyes, but a small smile plays on his lips. Then, with a gentle shake of his head, he begins, "Before it was a dinosaur—"

"Maisie!" Jake suddenly interrupts, excited. "You have to see this!" he says, tugging on one of the books on the large book-case. Without warning, the top half of a door swings open, while the bottom remains in place.

"Woah! That is so cool!"

"Right? Dad made it so I can keep my door closed when he's working but still see him while I'm playing."

Ethan just shrugs. "It was a compromise."

He pops the lever on the bottom half and swings that open too, but the other room is dark and I can't see inside it yet.

"Alright, last room for the night before we head to bed."

"The library!" Jake exclaims, and I follow him in, my jaw nearly hitting the floor. This room is everything a dedicated reader could ever want and more. There's a desk in the corner that looks to be Ethan's, plush couches off to the side with a view of the fields.

"Do you have a photographic memory?" I ask Ethan, and

he laughs again. I've heard him laugh more tonight than I have in a decade, and each time it fills my soul.

He's quiet, looking around, then, almost nervously, he asks, "Do you like it?"

My hand lifts, as if to touch his arm, but I stop myself. "I love it. It's... everything," I say sincerely, feeling a warmth in my chest that I thought I had long forgotten. The way he smiles in return, it's so genuine that it sends warning bells echoing in my head, reminding me to tread carefully even if I so desperately wish to cling to this fleeting moment of closeness.

Trying to create the distance my anxiety so desperately craves, I add, "You executed the vision perfectly. I'm so glad the hill gets the honor it deserves and that Jake gets to grow up here with you."

His smile instantly slips a fraction as he stares at me like he's dissecting every word, every nuance behind what I say, his eyes intense and focused. I feel that weight, and suddenly, I start to fidget, twisting my fingers anxiously, breaking eye contact for a moment.

When I look back, his eyes are locked onto mine again, like he's weighing something inside his head. I notice the slight twitch in his jaw and the way his hands curl into fists, then relax again. I almost cave under the pressure—or at least I want to ask more, get him to say what he's really thinking—but before I can, he just shakes his head slowly, like he's dismissing it all, then abruptly shifts the subject.

"Last thing," he says, voice calm but serious. "Hidden underneath the geodes around the house are security buttons. All you have to do is push one of those, and it'll send an alert to me, Hayes, and the whole team."

I glance around quickly, noticing at least three of those spectacular freestanding geodes, each shimmering with a different vivid color—blue, purple, and amber—like tiny galaxies trapped in rock.

"They're all over?" I ask, voice a little hesitant, my gaze flickering toward the double doors leading out into the hallway.

"Every room," Jake volunteers, yawning at the same time. "But you gotta be really careful. Only touch them if it's an emergency..." He trails off and leans into Ethan's side, eyes heavy again.

"And on that note," Ethan smiles down at him lovingly, "it's time for bed."

Then, just like that, I find myself sleeping in Ethan's bed.

Nine hours ago, it had been seven years since I had talked to him. If you'd told me even six hours ago that I'd end up here tonight, I would have laughed in your face. Yet, here I am. Crossing the line of all lines and knowing there wouldn't be any way I could go back to the cold shoulder after this.

After a quick stop back in Jake's room, where he helped Jake pick out his own pajamas. Ethan led us into his room, going for his closet and grabbing some clothes for me to borrow. When he comes out, he's carrying sweatpants and an oversized shirt—both of which I will surely swim in.

He points toward the ensuite bathroom and once again I'm flabbergasted. Obviously, I knew he had money, but did he spare a single expense on this house? Probably not. I could stare at the luxurious bathroom for hours, but I know they're waiting for me to change.

Don't think about it, just put the clothes on, and head to bed. Tomorrow is a fresh day where I can go home and pretend this never happened.

When I return, it's to find Jake and Ethan watching Bluey in bed. Jake is nearly half asleep and doesn't look up from his cartoon, but I can feel Ethan's gaze on me the entire time I make my way to the other side of his bed.

Ohmygod. What on earth am I doing here?

It's quiet for a few minutes, my thoughts spiraling as we both lie there in silence. When I finally muster the courage to look over, I see Jake sleeping peacefully between us.

Ethan notices as well and shuts off the TV, and as my eyes adjust, I notice the moonlight flooding the room. I hadn't realized it before, but it must be full— fitting for how tonight has turned out.

Ethan's facing Jake, lying on his side, and when I turn to look, I catch him staring at Jake, lightly running his thumb over his forehead.

"She said she didn't want him. Didn't want kids. I thought the settlement would be enough, but I should've known she was crazy."

"Did you guys date for very long?" I ask, the question that's been eating away at me for the last five years finally slipping out.

"We didn't date at all." His voice cracks, and all I want to do is reach over and comfort him, but I hold back. Too many lines have already been crossed.

"It was one night. Just one, Maisie. I swear."

"What happened?"

"We met at a party. I was having a rough day and decided to drink. I blacked out pretty quickly, and the next morning, she was in my bed. I didn't see her again until she showed up on my doorstep, eight months pregnant."

"Wow." It's not much, but it's all I can think to say.

Of course, I'd heard the rumors and had assumed something like this had gone down, but I'd also heard crazy things— she was a crackhead, some kind of royalty, or that she died in childbirth. Small-town rumors really know no bounds, and I tried to tune it all out.

"After the paternity test, she said she'd give me full custody and walk away."

"For how much?" I can't help but ask. I doubt she'd do that just out of the kindness of her heart.

"Half a million."

"That's it?!" I nearly screech, and Jake twitches beside us, almost waking up at my outburst.

Ethan lets out a light chuckle, which rocks the bed, but luckily, it settles Jake back into sleep almost instantly.

"It's absurd, right? Technically, I was in a signing year. They had just opened up contracts and were offering me double my rookie year. She could've had me for millions."

"Why didn't she?"

"My lawyer. He fought pretty dirty, but she came to us first, saying she didn't want him at all. Made it crystal clear that she wanted out. Duncan pretty much told her she could take the five hundred thousand, or we'd file for full custody and prove she was an unfit parent, which would blow up in the media. She didn't even want anyone to know she was pregnant —she had dreams of being an influencer or some shit."

"So she took it and that was it?"

"Yep," he sighs. "Until today."

"Did she contact you after she took him?"

"Texts—she wanted three million to an offshore account."

"And she thought she would get away with that? How?" I'm not exactly a tech-y person but how on earth does she think she wouldn't get caught with making that kind of demand over a text.

Ethan pauses, his brow furrowing as he thinks it through. "I don't know. She probably thought—I don't really know. If Luke hadn't been there when I got her texts... I would've sent the money that second just to get him back. I know that would've been the wrong move, but I wasn't thinking rationally."

"Probably not the best move... but, you're a good dad, E. You'd do anything for him, and that's evident to everyone around you."

"Yeah.." He sighs so heavily that I can tell he's about to say something I'm not sure I'm ready to hear. "I wish it ended there but that's not all. She's threatening you now. When I had to talk to Luke—it was because she texted. She's coming after you."

"Me?!"

"Luke's on it. He's having his team, as well as the EFSC guys, look into it. The problem is, she's using an 'unplugged' phone. So far, it's been untraceable—but they're hoping Lincoln will be able to figure it out."

"I— I just don't get it. She's coming after me because I saved Jake?" It makes no sense. None at all. And what's even weirder? That she tried to befriend me. She became such a regular in my line that I saw her a few times a week. And while yes, my coffee is the best in town, it always felt like she was trying to be my friend. But why? Spend a day in this town, and the gossips would have already spread that Ethan and I weren't even talking.

Ethan doesn't answer right away. Just keeps quiet so long I start to think he's fallen asleep.

Then, in that quiet, intense voice, he finally says, "She's coming after you because she knows I'm still in love with you."

My stomach drops, and I barely manage to whisper, "What?"

Suddenly, he's sitting up more, really looking at me. "Do you want to have this conversation tonight? Because I have a feeling you're still spiraling, trying to catch up to how everything's changed tonight."

"I—I don't know."

"How about I talk tonight, and you can have the time you need to process?"

"Okay..." I nod, feeling overwhelmed by how suddenly everything's happening. My eyes are already starting to sting, like I can feel the tears coming, even though I don't want to admit it.

"Maisie—I've been in love with you since before I even knew what that word meant. You weren't just my best friend; you were *everything* to me. I don't—" He pauses, taking a deep breath, and I feel like I stop breathing, waiting for him to keep going. "I don't know what changed. What I did to hurt you, or why you left and refused to talk to me. But it gutted me. The last twelve or so years, I've felt hollow, insecure, confused—but I never doubted my love for you. I'm not saying I didn't have flings or hookups in between, but I never wanted any of that in the way I've always wanted you. The night before graduation? The night we sat up here? I told you I'd build this house for you. I told you I'd be back in a few years, and I told you there wasn't anyone I could see myself being with besides you."

Without thinking, I let it slip, "I never said *you* did anything. Never said *you* hurt me." *I didn't say anything to anyone.*

"Then what the fuck happened, Maisie? Because something changed when I left the grad party early." *Yeah, Ethan, something did. Something I'll never be able to tell you about, something I can't even admit to myself.*

"I—" My voice trails off, unwilling to say anything else that might give away more than I already have. "I can't talk about this. Goodnight, Ethan."

"Maisie—come on, talk to me."

"Goodnight." He must sense the finality in my tone because, finally, he drops it.

Chapter Fourteen

Maisie

Bonfire After The Graduation Party

Twelve years prior—

"Liv! Mais!" Olivia and I both look up as Leilani and our other friend Kyle pull up next to us. They've already changed out of their dresses and into more casual clothes, ready for the bonfire.

"Want a ride?" Leilani yells through the open window.

Olivia glances at me, shrugging like she's asking if it's okay but also saying she's fine with it. Somewhere in my head, I hear my dad's voice warning me to never go somewhere I can't get out of quickly, but at least I've got Olivia with me.

"Sure! But we need to grab our stuff first." We'd both packed extra clothes earlier—just in case something like this came up—and I left mine in Olivia's Jeep. We hurry over, grab our bags, and I reach in, pulling out some shorts and a shirt. I hesitate for a second, trying to decide if I should grab anything else, but I end up leaving the bag behind so I don't have to carry it all night.

By the time we reach the bonfire, there are already at least a dozen vehicles parked around—tailgates facing inward towards the fire in the middle.

The sun's long gone, and all that's left is the glow of the large fire and a few trucks pulling in. The place is alive with laughter, music, and the crackling of wood as it burns.

People are wandering around—some just leaving the grad party, others from high school who graduated a few years before us but aren't old enough for the bars yet.

"Oh my god," Olivia whispers, nudging me with her elbow and pointing toward a tall guy with sandy hair and a confident smile plastered across his face. "Dan's here..."

"You're going over there," I say, kind of matter-of-fact. She's had a crush on Dan forever, but because he graduated before us, he's been off-limits—or at least not really on her radar.

"I can't!"

"Olivia, are you kidding me?"

"Maisie, please don't make me go alone."

I sigh. "Come on, Amanda's over there, and I wanted to talk to her about her schedule at COCC anyway." A lot of our classmates are sticking around here, going to community college in Bend. Ethan's college is one of the furthest, but I heard one of the guys named Jeff is heading to Yale. Other than that, most are staying in Oregon or nearby.

Dan looks up as we walk over and barely glances at me with a quick nod and smile—only eyes for Olivia, totally locked on her. I could almost laugh. She has absolutely nothing to worry about in that department. He looks practically in love already.

After I chatted with Amanda a bit, I do a quick check on

Olivia to see her sitting next to Dan on the tailgate of his truck. When she makes eye contact, I send her a quick wink and then settle myself on the tailgate of Ethan's friend Brandon's Toyota Tacoma, and listen to the sounds of friends and laughter blend into a warm, familiar hum.

It's not long before Leilani stumbles over with a drink in her hand. "Maisie! Want a beer?" She asks with a grin, practically shoving the bottle into my hand before disappearing back into the crowd on the other side of the fire.

"Not really," I answer, setting it down next to me. By the look of Leilani, I'm guessing Olivia or I will need to be her sober driver later.

The fire sparks to life as someone tosses a big stick onto it, and I get distracted watching the flames dance. My mind drifts to Ethan, and a wave of anxiety hits me hard in the gut. I keep imagining him hanging out with Alexandra—are they laughing and playing cards? Or maybe watching a movie together? Are they all cozied up on the couch? Does Alexandra have feelings for him? How could she not? Or, maybe she doesn't—maybe she sees him just as a brother. Still, Ethan bailed on one of his last nights here to be with her, and they'll be at the same college soon. It's enough to make my stomach twist with anxiety.

As I glance around, trying to find someone I can talk to before I spiral anymore, I look over to see the identical version of Dan with a woman currently straddling him. Typical, Levi. I have no idea who he is making out with, but I will say she has the most unique shade of auburn hair I've ever seen. Or maybe it's the reflection from the fire, but either way, it practically glows.

Levi's always been the troublemaker twin—up for a little chaos but still stands for the same values as his brother and their dad. Considering their dad's the sheriff, that moral high ground is pretty high. If anything, I'm surprised they're even here. Unless, of course, Levi dragged Dan along, and Dan's just here to keep him from crossing any lines. Judging by how comfortably that girl had her tongue down Levi's throat, I'd say Dan's a little too busy himself to keep track of Levi, though.

I wonder if Alexandra has her tongue down Ethan's throat...

Scottie, the guy who moved to town a few years ago, saunters over and plops down on the tailgate next to me. He's athletic, short and stocky—played football, but not very well. I knew he had some issues with Ethan in the past, but Ethan always played it down or just ignored it. It usually came down to jealousy, mixed with a few eye rolls whenever Ethan's name was brought up. But Ethan, with all his confidence, just brushed it off.

"Hey," Scottie says, nodding toward the bonfire. "You here with Liv?"

"Yeah, she's a bit distracted over there," I reply with a laugh, pointing in their direction.

"Distracted is one way to put it," he quips, rolling his eyes good-naturedly. "But they do look good together."

"Definitely," I agree, feeling the flickering warmth of the fire on my skin. Olivia deserves somebody like Dan, smart and charming. It's nice to see her happy for once.

We both sit back for a moment, letting the distant laughter and music drift through the night air. I glance over at Scottie and catch him watching me out of the corner of his eye, a playful smirk creeping onto his lips.

A text comes through, vibrating in my pocket, and my heart beats faster hoping it's Ethan.

Only when I pull my phone out to look, I see it's from Olivia. I glance up at her, and notice she looks guilty—like she's about to ask for a favor or do something reckless.

"No Flacco tonight?" Scottie asks when I put my phone down, his tone shifting a little. "Surprised he's not here, making sure no one gets too close."

The knots in my stomach only twist even more, and I can't help but frown, a mix of confusion and irritation bubbling up inside me. "What do you mean by that?"

He shrugs, taking a sip from his energy drink. "I just figured he'd try to kick my ass for talking to you. You two together?"

I hesitate, the memory from last night flashing—how that kiss felt electric, then how weird things had gotten today with all the distance. I start to say, "We're—" but then I catch myself. The words get tangled, and I grope for something that sounds honest but not too much. "It's complicated," I finally manage. "He leaves in a few days."

"Yeah—heard about that. Me too, actually."

"Where are you headed?" I ask, shifting my focus back to Scott.

"Fort Leonard Wood, Missouri. Leaving on Monday."

"What? Why?" I ask, honestly surprised.

"Army," he says, voice steady, and he holds my gaze a little longer than usual. I get the feeling he's trying to impress me or something. And while yes, that's incredible that he's joining the Army, I can't help but feel a pang of awkwardness at the interaction.

"I had no idea. That's pretty cool, Scottie," I say, trying to keep it light.

Just then, Leilani walks back and plops down between us with a bright, carefree smile. "Guys, you won't believe what just happened! Zach got his mom's minivan stuck on the way out here. And then when they tried to pull it out, they broke her bumper off!" she exclaims, clearly amused by the situation. I can't help but laugh at the image of Zach struggling with a minivan in the mud, feeling grateful for the distraction from Scottie's intense demeanor.

"Sounds like a tragedy," Scottie quips, chuckling lightly.

Soon, our little circle grows—several friends join in, laughter and shouts of excitement filling the night. They start dogging on Ethan, asking where he is, and each question feels like a small weight pressing down on my chest. I struggle to come up with a reply each time—just feeling that tug of longing I can't quite shake.

The night drags on, and I start to feel restless.

I glance over at Leilani, considering suggesting we head out, but when I go to find her, she's deep in conversation with Brandon, completely lost in her own world. Kyle's sitting nearby, looking bored out of her mind, but I know she's just letting Leilani have her moment.

"Hey, do you need a ride back to town?" Scottie offers, leaning against the truck with that easy grin of his. "I'm sober, I promise."

I've only seen him with an energy drink, but still, I hesitate.

"Uhm, let me just check with the girls first—see if they're ready."

Leilani barely even looks up at me, her hand gripping Brandon's arm like she's trying to keep him close. Kyle rolls her eyes but shakes her head and laughs anyway.

"I take it y'all aren't ready to leave?" I ask, trying to keep my tone easygoing.

Leilani looks at us with these big, pleading eyes—like she's begging us to stay. "I'm not... but..."

"No, it's fine," I cut in before she can finish. "I've got a ride, just wanted to check with you first."

Kyle gives me a worried look. "Are you sure? I can take you, then swing back."

"It's all good—just a quick ride to get my car," I say, trying to sound chill, even though inside, I've got this weird feeling gnawing at me, like something's just off.

Her eyes narrow a little while she draws out the word, "Okay," but besides that, she doesn't say anything.

I say my goodbyes, turning to head out, but only a few steps away from his truck, my foot catches on a rock, and I stumble forward. Instantly, Scottie's arm slips around my waist, steadying me against him. I can feel the warmth radiating from him as I regain my balance.

"Careful there," he says, his voice low and amused, a smirk in his voice.

Once I'm steady, he helps me the rest of the way. I settle onto the worn cloth seat, itchy beneath me, as the engine rumbles and we start bumping down the dirt road. As we drive, I catch Levi giving me a long, disapproving look before shaking his head at Scottie—like a silent warning I'm trying not to feel.

A knot tightens in my stomach, a strange kind of unease creeping in, whispering that I should get out, that I should have accepted the offer from Kyle. But I push that feeling aside, telling myself it's just a ride.

Scottie turns up the radio, and for a moment, I'm lost in the music, but the tug of doubt lingers, shadowing my thoughts as we speed off into the night.

Chapter Fifteen

Ethan

I woke up in a haze this morning, though the reality was that I hadn't really slept at all. My mind was a relentless whirlwind, replaying the chilling details of how my son had been kidnapped. It had only been, what, a few hours that he was gone? Yet, each moment, every fear, was etched into my memory like a scar. And then, against all odds, the girl I had loved for so long—My Fierce Maisie—had rescued him. She had stepped into that nightmare and brought him back to me, as if it wasn't the bravest, dumbest thing she's ever done. As if she was meant to be the one to do it, as if it was the only thing that would truly bring us back together.

Still, a nagging intuition whispers at me, like I don't have her back fully. I've always known she was hiding something about graduation night, but it wasn't until last night when I heard the devastation in her voice that I realized I had it all wrong. Her words replay, "I never said you did anything. Never said you hurt me." Which means someone else hurt her. Someone out there is haunting her, ensuring she keeps her secrets behind an impenetrable veil. And I'm going to figure out who and end them.

My phone's shrill ring cuts through the fog of my thoughts, jarring me awake. The caller ID flashes "Hayes"—my friend, the man I desperately need by my side in this chaos. I push myself out of the bed I share with Maisie and Jake, careful not to disturb them as they lie sleeping peacefully, blissfully unaware of the storm brewing in my mind.

Quietly, I padded to the kitchen.

"Hey," I greeted as soon as I answered, my voice rough from the lack of rest. "Need your help."

"Anything you need, man. You already know that." Hayes said, his tone serious. "Jake doing okay?" Hayes is a new dad but I've always appreciated his thoughtfulness toward Jake. He practically walked in when Jake was still a baby and became an honorary uncle from the beginning.

"He's alright. Shaken up, but he, uh—he insisted Maisie spend the night here." I can't help the small smile and shake of my head as I admit, "and that we all have a sleepover in my room."

A half chuckle and shocked breath came from him, "Damn, who knew kindergarteners made the best wingmen? Should've enlisted his help years ago."

"Had I known—I would have." I say with a resigned sigh.

"How are you holding up? Never been in your shoes, but that was a fucked-up night, Ethan."

"Honestly?" I took a breath, leaning against the cool marble counter. "I'm not okay. Jake was kidnapped, and I'm still working to wrap my head around it. That kind of fear... it changes everything." The weight of my words felt heavier than I anticipated.

"That's—" I hear the breath come out of him as he considers his next words, "More than understandable," he replied gently. "We've got your back. Whatever you need and want us to do. The guys have been working with Luke since last night. Lincoln's already working on the cyber side. Coop and Delta are putting in the groundwork and running through everything that happened. We're going to find her."

I wish I could say the sincerity of his tone calmed my fraying nerves, but I only feel more anxious. "Thanks. I, uh— haven't talked to Luke yet this morning. I take it there's no lead?"

"Not yet. They went through the cabin house but couldn't find anything else. Lincoln's been combing through the footage of the cabins on that road and further down, seeing if they can get the vehicle she left in, but so far, he hasn't found anything."

"Fuck." I groan, tugging at the hair at my nape. "I want a full detail on Maisie and Jake. The system at the house is good, but maybe you could see if Lincoln can beef it up? I can't have anything like this happening again. Whatever the cost."

"What about Maisie's house? Is she staying with you or going back there?"

"If I have it my way? She's moving in here." *Forever.*

"Considering you haven't had it your way in a while when it comes to her..."

I pause, considering his words. "Send Lincoln there too, I guess."

"Consider it done. He's pretty busy, though. She'll need to stay with you for a few days until he can get there." And I swear I can hear the smirk in his tone. *Apparently, I have two wingmen.*

I nodded, though he couldn't see me. "Thanks, man. I appreciate it."

"You're doing the right thing." Hayes assured me. "Call y'all when I know something."

As we wrapped up the call, I moved to the fancy coffee

machine that took me nearly a year to learn how to use properly. It's one of those high-end models I once heard Maisie gushing about to Olivia. Her voice was so full of longing as she described how luxurious it would feel to have that kind of coffee at home, I ordered it online, right then and there. Hearing her passion for the little things always struck a chord with me—thus the reason this house is basically a shrine to all the things Maisie loves.

I might have looked like a fool, but I couldn't stop soaking in every detail I could find about her. It was idiotic, I knew. The voice of reason in my head warned me I was crossing the line, that I needed to let her go before someone discovered just how obsessive I'd become. But how could I let her go? Not when I knew, with every fiber of my being, that she was meant to be mine.

Still lost in thought, my back rests against the edge of the kitchen counter as I stare at the cup filling, the rich aroma filling the kitchen.

"Is that a Miele?" Maisie's soft gasp infiltrated the kitchen, snapping me back into reality, her presence both a balm and a spark.

Spinning around, I see her eyes wide with excitement, staring at the obsidian black machine.

"It is—"

"Oh my god! Can I use it?!"

Smiling, I gesture with an open hand.

She approached the espresso machine with an ease that surprised me, deftly tapping buttons and adjusting the settings. I'd been the one who took a crash course on how to operate it, yet here she was, navigating it like she owned it.

"You've never even used one before, have you?" I questioned, raising an eyebrow at her as I did my best to not drift toward her.

She looked up, the hint of a grin breaking through the remnants of last night's chaos. "Surprisingly, my instincts seem to be on point this morning," she replied, a playful spark igniting in her eyes. A moment later, a rich, alluring aroma filled the air, one that somehow smelled even better than my own previous brew. She held her cup to her nose, inhaling deeply, a mixture of contentment and joy washing over her features.

When she finally met my gaze, my heart twisted painfully in my chest. The ache of wanting her darted through me like electricity. Her disheveled appearance—makeup smudged, chestnut hair piled high in a messy bun—only accentuated her raw beauty. She's still my beautiful, fierce Maisie, the one I had missed more than I could admit.

"I'm so sorry," she mumbled, quickly vanishing her smile. "I didn't mean to... after everything that happened last night."

"It's all good," I assured her, fighting the urge to scoop her up in my arms. I wanted to hold her tight and shield her from the world, but I also didn't want to overstep. "I'm just glad you're enjoying it as much as I hoped you would."

Her expression shifted to one of shock, but she quickly covered it by taking a sip of her fresh brew. A soft moan escaped her lips as she savored the rich flavor, and I grunted in response, struggling to suppress the thoughts racing through my mind, ignited by the seductive sound she had just made. *Too late, you're done for.*

Maisie moved to sit in one of the tall chairs at the horseshoe-shaped kitchen counter, and I leaned against the opposite side. She looked at me, her brow slightly furrowed as she stirred her coffee. "So—have you talked to anyone since last night?"

I sighed, acknowledging the weight of the situation. "I spoke to Hayes. They haven't found out anything yet. I hired the EFSC team to put a security detail on you and Jake."

Her eyes widened briefly, and for a moment, I braced for her to push back. Instead, she nodded thoughtfully. "I think that's good. Obviously, we don't know what she's capable of."

I felt a sliver of relief but knew the conversation was far from over. "Lincoln will be updating your apartment security system in a few days, and I need you to stay with me until it's done."

She opened her mouth to protest. "I can't just—"

"Maisie," I interrupted gently but firmly. "You need to be safe. That means you either stay here or with Hayes and Charlie, or even Drew and Olivia."

She crossed her arms, a playful twinkle returning to her eyes. "I could also stay in the frat house? Four Navy SEALs and a barista. I'm sure there's a—"

A flash of jealousy surged through me, a sudden blaze that almost took me by surprise. "Don't even finish that fucking sentence, Maisie," I demanded, my voice sharper than I intended.

Realizing her comment might have struck a nerve, she backpedaled quickly, raising her hands in a placating gesture. "I'm kidding, I'm kidding. I appreciate you letting me stay here —and use your Miele."

A slight smile crept onto my lips at that, even as my stomach knotted with all the emotions swirling around us. "You're safe here, and that's what matters most."

And as she sipped her coffee, the air filled with something electric—intense, conflicting, yet undeniably familiar. I've always known she belonged here, but seeing her here is an entirely new healing touch to my heart. Now I only need to figure out how to get her to stay here permanently. And somehow, I know it means figuring out the secret she's keeping.

Chapter Sixteen

Maisie

"You're safe here, and that's what matters most." Ethan said it as if it wasn't everything my heart had wanted to hear since the moment I let him go. I hadn't even known the impact it would have on me—the complete chokehold it had on my fears and anxieties. He's always been the fixer to my problems, and it's the reminder I needed of why I did let him go. He never would've left for training camp had he known what happened.

That's why I was grateful when a few moments later, Jake came stomping into the kitchen—tousled hair and bright eyes, ready to pull me out of my tangled thoughts.

"You're still here!" he yelled, throwing his arms around me.

"I wouldn't leave without saying goodbye, little razz," I say, briefly glancing at Ethan, making sure it's okay that I'm practically holding his son in my arms.

What I don't expect is to almost get knocked on my ass when I catch Ethan already grinning back at me. We've been so serious and quiet around each other for so long—his smile, though, it does something to me, like it's reviving my soul and sending me somewhere I really shouldn't go.

"Can we have pancakes for breakfast?" Jake asks.

"I think we can swing that," Ethan says, already moving around the kitchen.

It feels so natural, being here with Jake next to me, sipping on one of the best coffees I've ever had. So natural, it's almost like I see it—the house Ethan's built, filled with everything he knows I could want. Every nook and cranny reflects his intentions for us, and with each painstaking detail, it's starting to threaten my resolve further. I could see myself here, see myself living here and being part of this beautiful family. The sense of familiarity and love enveloping me so fully, yet rather than comforting me, it flares my anxiety.

I can't.

I can't be with Ethan.

Not after everything that happened, how I handled all the situations I was forced in to. My baggage is far too heavy to bring into this beautiful home and upset the life he's built. If Ethan knew how truly broken I really am, he wouldn't want me in the same way. I'm not the fierce Maisie he thought I was—a warrior bravely navigating life's waters. Instead, I'm more like a ghost haunting the edges of a beautiful dream, longing to reclaim what seems lost.

"I need to go into Maisie's today!" I blurted out, accidentally interrupting Jake telling Ethan what he wants on his pancakes. Cringing, I add, "And grab stuff from my place..."

Ethan's neck practically snaps as he looks at me and my outburst. Then he nods once and grabs his phone from the edge of the counter. "I'll call Hayes."

I start to move around the kitchen, using the things Ethan had already gotten out and finding the other ingredients without problem. Once again, I'm so thankful for Jake, who doesn't let a second go by without talking. He chatters on about the end of the school year being next week and all the fun activities they'll get to do.

After a few minutes, Ethan comes back in and quietly lets me know that Hayes has Liam and Delta rotating my babysitting services, and Liam is up first today. A true blessing because I'm not sure that I could face Leo right now. Not that anything ever happened between us, but it still feels like the promise of a dance after the rodeo was cheating on my non-existent relationship with Ethan. Especially after sleeping in the same bed with him last night.

Plus, Liam is basically a giant teddy bear, even down to the not talking—a comforting presence in a chaotic world. He opens doors like it's his duty and tips too generously on his black coffees, his kindness spilling out in all directions. He watches out for everyone, protective and attentive without uttering too many words. Which means I'm grateful that today, he's the one by my side.

I finish making the pancakes, and as I'm plating them, a chime in the house rings a delicate melody, and I look to Ethan for an explanation. His hands grip the edge of the granite countertop like he's trying to break it, muscles strained as he stares down at it.

Then with a heavy puff of air, he says, "They're here" and leaves to open the front door.

"Sweet! Lincoln is so cool! He taught me sooo many cheats for Mario."

"Did he?" I say as I try to peek at Ethan in the doorway. He stands there, shoulders squared and posture firm, only a few inches shorter than Liam, but the tension radiating off Ethan is palpable. Lincoln, just as tall but lanky, looks like a twig next to these two towering figures, yet he possesses the same "don't fuck with me" aura that effortlessly fills the space.

Jake and I continue to eat our pancakes, only instead of the chatterbox he was, he's being quiet, like he too is trying to listen to the conversation.

"Tell me more about what you want to do this summer! Think you'll get to swim in the pool at Ellie's?"

He nods, but doesn't say anything. I scramble to think of more things to say, but thankfully a moment later the guys come in. Lincoln is all smiles as he greets Jake with a high-five. "Dude! I heard you made it to Petal Isles?!"

Jake's mood instantly shifts and he nods with big eyes, his mouth full of the last bite.

"You'll have to show it to me when you're done eating."

"I'm done! I'm done! Dad, can I go get it?"

Ethan nods, "Sure big guy."

Jake set his plate in the sink and tore off toward his room.

Lincoln's hand falls on my shoulder as a half pat, half squeeze. "Sure I'm not the first one to tell you this—but—you did good, Mais."

"Thanks," I say, feeling the heat rise to my cheeks like it did last night.

He nods and then starts walking around the kitchen, chatting briefly with Liam about the security system; Ethan's attention is fixed on them, his expression unreadable. I can see the undercurrents of concern flickering in his eyes, and it makes my heart ache.

Finally, Liam looks at me and gives me a chin tip—his silent cue that it's time to go. "Ready?" he asks gently, his voice raspy but somehow reassuring. I nod, but my throat tightens, swallowing around the lump that threatens to spill over. I need to get out of this house before I do something dumb like give in and stay forever.

Liam is his usual quiet self as he drives us toward the hut.

His eyes are on a swivel, though, like he's prepared for someone to jump out of nowhere and come for us—well, me.

He lets me work in the back, prepping as much as I can for a few days of work. Ashleigh already offered to come in earlier this week to help bake so that I can take a few days off, but I still want to have everything ready for her. Normally on a Sunday I'd spend the entire day locked away in here, creating new recipes or prepping, but I'm already anxious to get back to the house. An annoying conundrum, considering I couldn't get out of there fast enough. *Is this what it feels like to implode? I'm losing my mind.*

Four hours later, I'm feeling better about being gone a few days and let Liam know I'm ready to go to my apartment.

We make the short drive, and he pulls into the spot I normally park in, but he doesn't make a move to get out; he only stares at my door like he's trying to use x-ray vision to see inside.

I reach for the handle as he says, "Wait."

I snap my attention to him but he's only glaring at the door. Then I notice the gun in his hand and my eyes widen. I look back at the door, terror running through me. *What on earth does he see that I don't?*

Hayes's voice fills the truck, and I realize he must have called him. "Yeah?"

"Maisie's apartment, now," his voice all gravel and steel.

The line goes dead, but I don't have the courage to look at Liam.

Within two minutes, I heard the telltale sign of Cooper's Durango. It had some sort of supercharged engine that sounds like it's about to burst through the walls.

Cooper and Leo, have their guns drawn as they walk up the steps to my tiny apartment, looking like they've done this a million times. If it wasn't so terrifying, this would one hundred percent be movie worthy.

Liam hasn't moved an inch, yet I guarantee he is seeing everything going on around us.

Cooper barely touches the door with his toe and it opens up fully, as if it wasn't shut or locked like I know it was when I left yesterday. How the hell did Liam see that from down here?

They both go in, and then a few breaths later come out, and walk back down.

Liam reaches for his handle as I ask, "can we?"

He nods and I get out as well.

Leo approaches me first, giving me a quick hug. "It's clear, but it's—" he drawls off, and I look at Cooper who finishes for him. "Fucked up."

Without thinking, I rush up the stairs to see my destroyed small apartment. Everything is turned upside down, with broken glass and furniture scattered everywhere. The sense of violation washes over me, sending me to a place I've tried so hard to get over. It's not the same, but I can feel the panic attack starting to creep in. Leo's arm goes around my waist to help support me, but it feels like a lead weight that I can't shake off as I struggle to catch my breath.

It's a trigger.

I'm triggered; that's all.

Breathe, Maisie.

Only I can't; *His arm is around me, supporting me, helping me.*

Spots begin to fill my vision, the dizziness overtaking me, and then there's nothing.

Chapter Seventeen

Maisie

The Drive Home From The Party

Twelve Years Prior—

Scottie takes the familiar road back to town, but he's driving much slower than normal. I don't necessarily mind; it's a beautiful night, and at least he isn't speeding. The stars sprinkle the sky like a scattered handful of diamonds, captivating yet somehow distant. But no matter how hard I try to soak in the scenery, I can't shake Ethan from my mind. Will he be disappointed in me for going to that bonfire? Maybe I should've just gone home. But then I'd be the girl waiting around for him, and I don't want to be that person. I don't want to let life pass me by while Ethan is doing his thing, and I'm stuck in limbo.

The rap music blares through the speakers, a rhythm I don't know, and words I can't grasp, and it only amplifies my spiraling thoughts. Will it actually work between Ethan and I? I can't even go one night without feeling like he's forgetting about me, or I'm betraying him. And we are supposed to go years of long distance?

Abruptly, Scottie pulls over to the side of the road, slowing to a stop in a random cut-out. I glance over at him, curious. He lifts his fingers off the steering wheel, peering at the dash with a look that seems confused, but there's something underlying there—an eerie tip to his mouth—as if he's trying *not* to smile.

My pulse quickens as I track him backing into a dirt road that stretches into the darkness. But the music is too loud as I lean in to ask, "What's going on?"

"Huh?" He turns his head towards me, and a flash of something flickers across his face.

"What's going on?" I repeat, raising my voice a bit as I reach to hit the volume knob, silencing the booming bass that fills the car.

"Oh, I don't know. Started losing power; might just be the —" He trails off, his voice lacking its usual confidence. "I'll check. One second, yeah?"

It seems innocent enough, but a pit begins to form in my stomach. Why did he pull down this side road? Being stuck in the middle of nowhere feels unnerving, especially with the night so late, and dark. Suddenly, I regret not grabbing the jacket my mom insisted I put in my bag. The chill creeps in on my bare shoulder, and I start to feel uneasy.

Scottie climbs out of the truck and pops the hood. I lean out my window, looking around, but the only thing I see is the inky blackness enveloping us, illuminated only by the headlights spilling onto the narrow dirt road. Why here? Anyone driving by would barely see us, and that thought sends a shudder through me. *But, it's Scottie.* He's not a creep. *Right?*

Minutes tick by slowly, the quiet only broken by the distant sound of crickets chirping. Then, unexpectedly, I hear the tail-gate pop down behind me. I jump at the noise, glancing over my shoulder to find nothing. Just as I turn back, his door swings open with a sudden force, and I scream.

"Shit, sorry! Didn't mean to scare ya. The lights are blinding me," he chuckles, cutting off the headlights. "Can you help me hold the flashlight?"

"Oh, yeah. Sure." I fumble with my seatbelt, my heart racing as I step out of the truck.

I pull out my phone, using it as a makeshift flashlight, standing over where Scottie is fiddling under the hood. I wish I knew even the basics of mechanics, feeling the weight of regret for not spending more time with my dad on the farm. That was always Margie's area, knowing how to fix just about anything. I try to be helpful, shining the light on whatever he asks for, even handing him tools as needed, but the whole situation feels increasingly awkward.

"Actually, I have a bigger wrench—" He interrupts our benign moment, and I feel a twinge of hope for my usefulness. "In my toolbox. Can you grab it?"

As I go to fetch the tool, I step down from the bumper and nearly tumble. His arm goes out and catches me around my waist like it had earlier. It should be comforting, but I feel his fingers grip my pelvic bone a little too tightly, and another shiver goes down my spine. The kiss comes out of nowhere, catching me off guard. A rush of panic floods my system, and I yank away, trying to break free.

He's suddenly everywhere as I try to get away, but he still has a hold of my waist, like it's glued to his hand. That doesn't stop me from pushing him away with all my strength, my heart pounding wildly in my chest. Somehow, we end up locked in a struggle, tumbling into the dirt. Fear rushes through my veins as I find myself pinned beneath him; the weight of his body grinding into me, freezing me in place. Tears slip down my cheeks, blurring my vision, and in that disorienting moment, I feel utterly trapped—my breath hitching in my throat—and I can't move. *But it's Scottie... Why is he doing this?*

His hands are everywhere, gripping at my shorts, trying to yank them down. Then, as if somehow summoned by my fear, another face is looming over Scottie's shoulder, Levi. In a blink, Scottie is being dragged off me with a force that sends shock-waves through my body.

Dust hits my face, and I try to breathe but choke on the particles in the air. It keeps coming, but I don't understand where it's coming from. It reminds me of when my dad would move cattle, and the dust would kick up in the corral—suffo-cating and blinding.

Then I'm being lifted by my shoulders and dragged back-wards. My feet scramble for purchase, but then I hear a girl's voice: "You're okay. It's okay. You're okay. I've got you."

She stops pulling, and I turn to see the woman from the party. Levi's truck headlights now shine on her and I'm once again taken aback by the color of her red hair. Now that I can see her face, I'm struck by how beautiful she is. Yet, her eyes are wild and filled with fear, probably a mirror image to my own.

I look back to where I just was and see the reason for the dust flying. Levi has Scottie pinned to the ground, much like Scottie just had me, but is pummeling his fist into his face.

The woman from the party starts yelling at Levi to stop. Only I don't want him to stop, and what does that say about me?

She runs to him and finally, he stops punching, his knuckles red and bloody. He shakes his head at Scottie, stands up and spits on him.

Levi's eyes meet mine, filled with a mixture of worry and resoluteness. In that instant, I realized the magnitude of what just happened. I trusted someone with such a simple task of driving me to town, and instead, he betrayed me. Had Levi not been there, I'd be lying in Scottie's place, battered and bruised, still frozen in fear.

And the saddest part about all of it, this only confirms one thing in my mind, I'm not the "fierce Maisie" Ethan believes me to be.

Chapter Eighteen

Maisie

Coming to outside of my apartment, I find myself sprawled on the cold ground, a blanket twisted beneath me like a lifeline. Levi's face hovers above, etched with concern, his features momentarily blurring in and out of focus. A fresh wave of panic surges through me as fragments of a night I would rather forget claw at the edges of my mind.

"Maisie, you're okay," he insists, his voice threading through the chaos in my head. "It's not that night. You're okay, Mais." The familiarity of his tone brings a flicker of recognition, but it struggles to break through the suffocating haze that's settled around me.

His arm still tightly grips at my waist, holding on to me.

My heart races violently, each beat reverberating like a drum, echoing in my ears louder than his words. The weight of anxiety crushes me, a merciless tide rising and pulling me down into a dark current of fear. I can barely hear him above the storm in my chest, each breath escaping in shallow gasps that only deepen the panic.

The dust particles fly in the air again, choking me.

As the seconds stretch into eternity, I grasp for something—anything—to tether me to this moment. I focus on Levi's face, the way his brow furrows in empathy, how his lips form reassuring smiles that don't quite reach my fraying nerves. *Older, he's older now.* The slight crinkles around the corner of his eyes, the wisdom in his gaze that speaks volumes without a word.

It isn't that night. You're okay, Maisie. I've got you. It isn't that night.

"Breathe, Mais," he urges, his tone soothing yet insistent. "In and out. Just like we practiced." I try to mimic his rhythm, though the first few attempts feel heavy and jagged, my body unwilling to cooperate. I want to fight against the panic, but it feels like battling shadows—each inhale seems to send me deeper into the abyss.

Gradually, I begin to catch more fragments of his words amidst the noise. "You're safe," he repeats, his firm yet gentle hands resting on either side of my face, grounding me in reality. The warmth of his touch seeps through the fog, a flicker of comfort anchoring me to the present. "Inhale... One, two, three, four. Hold your breath... One, two, three, four. Exhale... Four, three, two, one."

I concentrate, pouring all my energy into following his lead. He's helped me with this before; I know this; I've done it before. With each breath, I feel the edges of my panic softening. The storm within me, volatile and wild, begins to ease its grip just enough for clarity to seep back in.

"Focus on what you can feel." I tune back in, noticing the cool ground against my skin and my fingers scrabbling for a grip on the blanket. "Focus on what you can smell." The faint smell of grass overwhelms the remnants of my scattered thoughts as I try to breathe in the fresh air.

Slowly, I'm able to start breathing again, the rhythm settling into something more manageable, more real. Levi's gaze remains locked on mine, unwavering and patient, as though he's willing me to emerge from the shadows. I latch onto his reassurance, repeating his words silently in my mind.

It isn't that night. You're okay, Maisie. I've got you. It isn't that night.

"I'm okay. I'm okay." I breathe heavily and watch as Levi sits back on his heels, a small smile tugging at the corners of his lips. He's in his full medic uniform which means one of the guys must have called 911. *Can't wait to hear what the town has to say about this.*

"You are. You're okay." He quickly blinks, and I swear it looks like a tear glistens in his eye before he's able to blink it away, a silent acknowledgment of the depth of my struggle. One that Levi has seen firsthand, multiple times, albeit not in a long time.

Luke's face appears next to his and as I try to sit up, they both reach out to help me up a bit.

"Shit, Maisie. A panic attack?" His voice is all sorrow and worry. "You haven't had one in years." *I know, Sheriff Obvious.*

After that night, I started having night terrors and the occasional panic attack. My sister forced me into therapy. Luke spent days working on self-defense with me. And Levi, well, Levi helped me with simply breathing. None of them made me talk to them about what happened, but they all helped in their own way.

I look around and see Cooper on the phone, glancing back at me with worry as he tells whoever he's talking to what happened—either Hayes or Ethan. Then I look to Leo who is talking to the other paramedics. Then to Liam, and I swear the way he's looking at me, it's like he knows what happened that night.

"You want me to check your vitals here, or in the back?" Levi asks pulling my attention back to him.

"Here's good," I say offering out my arm.

As he gets to work, I suddenly feel exhausted. The last twenty-four hours have been too much. I just want to curl up in a ball and sleep for a week.

"Alright, you're slowly getting back to a normal range." Then before he stands up, quietly, so only I can hear, he says, "We *will* talk about this."

Before I can stand up, Ethan's booming voice comes from behind me. "Maisie!"

I turn around to see him literally running while carrying Jake over his shoulder, fireman style. A concerned expression wouldn't begin to cover the look on his face. He nearly collapses next to me, somehow setting Jake down, who wears the same terrified expression as his dad.

"Are you okay?" his eyes searching mine for any sign of distress.

"I'm just tired," I reply with a weak smile, but tears still fill my eyes.

Jake's arms go around me, and I pull him into my lap. "Uncle Luke called and said you fainted like one of those goats do!"

That yanks a laugh out of me. "I did... but I'm okay, Razzy. Levi helped me work on my breathing like we've practiced before, and I'm feeling better now."

Jake looks up at Levi with wide eyes, clearly confused. "You had to practice breathing before?"

Ethan tenses next to me, and I realize my slip-up.

Levi's smile doesn't waver as he looks at Jake, though. "Yep, it's part of the job. I can help people stay calm when they're feeling overwhelmed or anxious. It's important to know how to handle those situations." Ethan relaxes slightly, and I silently thank Levi for covering for me, although I have a feeling it won't be enough.

"What can we do?" Ethan asks, looking at me first and then Levi.

"I'll let Maisie decide that. She knows how to handle panic attacks."

"Can we just go to your house? I wasn't able to get any of my stuff, but maybe one of the girls can let me borrow some stuff."

He nods, pulling out his phone. "Group text. I'm sure we'll have a closet full by the time we get back."

Chapter Nineteen

Ethan

We pull into the driveway, and even the sight of my house doesn't do much to calm the chaos inside me. I still feel the echo of Luke's call rippling through my body. Twice in twenty-four hours, I've felt my heart leave my chest. At some point, I'm not sure how much more it can take.

The second I saw his caller ID, I knew. By the time I answered, I was already yelling for Jake to get to the truck. Luckily, he's quick for his age and was already in the truck when Luke said, "Something happened with Maisie." Because I would've had no problem hauling him up like he's still a toddler and throwing him in myself. But he buckled without a question and didn't ask a thing. My truck auto-connected, and I listened to Luke explaining—someone broke into her house, she saw the aftermath, and then she passed out. That was all the info he gave as I sped down the gravel road into town, silently apologizing to every worker on the ranch as dust flew at them, hard—I know they'd understand if they knew what happened. Hell, they'd be right behind me. The town's going to lose their minds when they find out someone's coming after Maisie—and honestly, I'm here for it.

We made the twenty-minute trip in fifteen, and I kept having to remind myself, again and again, to slow down because Jake was in the truck. By the time we got to her, she was already up, and Levi was hovering over her like a nervous mother hen. Yeah, that's his job— but I could see it in his eyes that there was more than him simply fulfilling his duty. He knows something. I can feel it in my bones—that whatever she's hiding, he's aware of it and even helped her work through it.

I put the truck into park and glance at her, sitting in the passenger seat.

She looks smaller, more frail, and utterly exhausted, yet she offers a small smile. "Would it be okay if I took a bath? Your tub looked like it was made for me." *That's because it was.*

I don't say that, though; I simply nod and glance back at Jake, who is unbuckling himself.

"Want to help me start dinner while Maisie relaxes?"

"Yes! What are we making? What's your favorite food, Maisie? Dad makes the best mac and cheese!"

"That sounds perfect! Are you sure you don't mind? I can help—"

I interrupt her before she can finish her sentence. "No worries, we've got it covered. Your mom said she left some clothes on the porch, and the girls said they'll bring some stuff over this evening."

She glances at the porch, swallowing hard, then nods. "Thank you." I see tears brimming in her eyes, but she opens the door and rushes up to the house before I can say anything else.

That was forty-five minutes ago, and she's still in there— bathing in my bathroom. The steam and warmth are separated from me by walls I feel are closing in. I want—no, need

—to be in there with her, demanding answers that swirl endlessly in my mind. *Why has Levi been the one helping her with her panic attacks? Why is she having them in the first place?*

My gut twists uncomfortably, hinting that whatever is haunting her is tied to that wretched night.

Jake's innocent comments try to pull me out of it, but I can't quite stay present for him. Then, finally, he asks, "Dad, is Maisie okay?" His wide eyes search mine—innocent but somehow perceptive. I flash him a forced smile, hiding the turmoil inside, hiding my own uncertainty. I see how worried he is, and I don't want to add to his burden, but all I can think about is how Levi's stepping into a role I should be filling. I want to scream, to demand that everyone step aside and let me push through the fog that has settled between us. But I can't— not right now. I've gotten this far with her, and while we've made progress, it stills feels fleeting.

Taking a deep breath, I focus on Jake, forcing myself to answer him thoughtfully and honestly. "She's going to be—but we should probably be patient with her. Panic attacks can be pretty scary for everyone involved," I finally say, my voice steady as I kneel to meet Jake's gaze.

"Is a panic attack what made her faint?"

"I think so— but I'm not entirely sure about the details. Maybe, in a few days, we can ask her if she's willing to share what happens when she has one and how we can help her if it happens again."

His worry eases just a little, and I tuck a loose strand of hair behind his ear, trying to convey reassurance I'm not entirely sure that I feel myself.

"Okay... I hope it doesn't happen again, though," he says softly.

Maisie steps into the kitchen with a much bigger smile than

usual, like she's pretending she's okay and using her customer service facade.

"Sorry that took so long. You didn't wait, did you?"

"It's not even done yet," Jake groans, plopping into the chair.

She glances toward the stove. "No boxes around here. It's all homemade, and should be ready soon."

"Oh," she nods approvingly, then grins at Jake. "It's sooo much better when it's not from a box. I think I can handle the wait."

By the time we eat, everything feels mostly normal. Jake's a natural at breaking the ice, making sure there's never a lull in conversation. Right now, he's enthusiastically recounting his T-ball practice from earlier in the week, his animated gestures making me smile despite the heaviness still weighing on my chest.

"Maisie, I hit a home run at the last game!" he declares, eyes practically sparkling with pride. "And Dad said I've got a game tomorrow!"

Maisie sits across from us, eating her pasta slowly. I catch her eye. "You able to come watch?"

My heart pounds a little at the thought of her there, and also the thought of her not there.

She hesitates for just a moment, gears turning in her mind. "Yeah, I'd like that," she finally replies, forcing a small smile.

Jake jumps up, throwing his fists in the air. "Awesome! It's gonna be so much fun! I might even hit another homer!"

We finish dinner, plates mostly cleared, and Jake bounds upstairs calling out, "Movie time!" I glance over at Maisie, who's running a hand through her damp hair. She looks slightly more relaxed but still carries that edge of uncertainty.

"Should I skip out tonight? I'm sure you have a guest room around here I could crash in," she asks light-heartedly.

"I'd really prefer if you didn't. It's been..." I weigh my words, trying to decide how deep to go. "It's been a lot. I'm already not going to sleep much, but having you breathing the same air as me would help."

She nods hesitantly, understanding the unspoken message. I need her with me—*I'm scared.* Despite everything, she's still the person I feel safest with, crave comfort from, and trust to hold me together.

We made our way to my bedroom, Jake already sprawled out across the bed, remote in hand and grinning from ear to ear. As the opening credits roll, I settle in next to him, and Maisie finds a spot on the far side, propped up by pillows.

"Two slumber parties in two days," Jake pipes up happily, and I can't help but laugh at how light and innocent a six-year-old's humor can be.

As the movie plays, I keep sneaking glances at Maisie, searching for some sign that she's okay—it's nearly impossible to tell what she's thinking as she zones out to the tv, though. *Is she tired? Will I get the chance to talk to her once Jake falls asleep, like I did last night? Will she open up to me?*

The longer the movie plays, the more desperate I feel to ask her the questions burning through my mind. *Why is she suffering from panic attacks? Why is Levi the one helping her? Is it just because he's a paramedic, or is there something more going on? Have I missed the signs?* I've never heard a rumor about Levi and Maisie around town, but maybe that's because even the town was protecting their secret.

Slowly, Jake's eyelids begin to droop, and I gently move him so that he's in a more comfortable sleeping position. "Just five more minutes," he mumbles, but it's not long before his head falls onto my shoulder, and I feel his breath slow into the steady rhythm of sleep.

I look over at Maisie, expecting to find her watching the

movie, but she's leaned back against the headboard, her eyes fluttering shut. She looks so peaceful, so at ease, I don't bother trying to wake her. I'm glad she feels safe enough to drift off, even if I feel a pang of disappointment in my chest.

I shut off the TV and sink back into the bed. I've waited this long for answers—I can wait a few more hours. At least I've got the two greatest loves of my life sleeping peacefully in this room with me. Tomorrow, I swear, I'll get to the bottom of everything—even if it means going to Levi about it.

Chapter Twenty

Ethan

Restless sleep doesn't begin to cover the night I had, and then I wake to a sudden jolt—the unmistakable elbow to my nose. Jake's soft voice trails behind it, "Sorry, Daddy."

"It's all good," I mutter, rubbing at the ache. My eyes flicker open, still blurred with sleep, and I see Jake's tousled hair as he stretches, innocence etched into his features.

"Where's Maisie?" His question has me sitting up on full alert, scanning the room like a hawk searching for its prey.

She pads out of the bathroom with one hand up and a toothbrush hanging out of her mouth.

"Present." Relief hits me instantly. I want to go to her and hug her, but I know that isn't the right move, not after I watched her shut down so completely last night.

I fall back into bed with an exaggerated sigh, star-fishing on the bed and nearly hitting Jake in the process. He only laughs and rolls his eyes, used to my dramatics by now.

"Breakfast?" This kid has a one-track mind, and it usually revolves solely around food.

"I was thinking about trying out a new muffin recipe today.

Any chance you'd be interested in helping me?" Maisie asks, and I watch as Jake's eyes light up as if she told him she were taking him to Disney and not baking muffins. *This.* This is what I've been wanting for so long and it's as if she's the missing piece that has now been found but refuses to fit.

My phone vibrates on the side-table, and I look to see Luke's caller ID. The happy moment broken as nerves settled in the pit of my stomach once again.

"S'up Luke?"

"Mind if Hayes and I drop by for a bit?" His tone reveals nothing, and rather than ask any questions, I let my head fall back onto the headboard with my eyes closed.

"By all means."

"Great, see ya in twenty." *Mother-fucking, fuck.*

"Everything okay?" Maisie asks softly, her voice gentle but hesitant. I open my eyes to find her watching me, her hands nervously fidgeting in front of her. I force a small smile.

"Luke and Hayes will be here soon."

Her eyes widen slightly, surprise flickering across her face, but she doesn't push for details. Instead, she turns toward Jake and smiles. "More taste testers for us," she says, giving Jake a quick wink before slipping back into the bathroom.

When she's done, I quicken my pace, shower, and by the time I'm downstairs, I find Maisie teaching Jake how to make muffins. I stand back, admiring the way she talks to him, how patient she is, and yet still animated. Jake is clearly loving every minute of her undivided attention and although I can't deny being jealous of my own child, I wouldn't change the way she treats him for anything.

I could stand here for hours watching her laugh and interact with him, but unfortunately the motion sensor dings, alerting me that someone is at the gate. Hayes and Luke both have the code to get in, so with a resigned sigh, I make my way to the front porch to wait for them—immediately regretting not having made a coffee to bring with me.

I perch in one of the rocking chairs, feeling the crisp breeze of a Central Oregon morning. Shortly it'll be close to seventy degrees, but right now, the cold night desert air lingers.

"Mornin'," Hayes greets first as he slides out of Luke's Sheriff truck. Luke waves with his freehand but has the other hand up to his ear.

"Haven't even had a coffee yet, Carrington."

"Well, maybe if you weren't gawking at a certain somebody all morning, you'd have one by now." *How does he know that?*

He laughs when I don't respond and he knows he got it right, taking a seat in the rocking chair next to me.

"How's August? I hope he's waking up every two hours just to keep you on your toes."

Hayes groans and tips his head back, "Is there a fourth month sleep regression or something? He went like three weeks sleeping mostly through the night and now he's back to waking up at least twice."

"Not sure—Jake didn't sleep a full night until he was over a year old. Thought he was trying to kill me."

Luke's door opens, and we both turn to watch him get out of his truck. Then, the front door swings open, and my attention immediately shifts to Maisie emerging—looking beautiful as ever, even with flour dusted on her clothes.

"Wow, you all look like you've aged a decade in the last few days," Maisie says with a sympathetic smile. "Want me to make some coffee?"

"Yeah, please," Hayes responds gratefully, rubbing his tired eyes. Luke nods. "All of it, really. As much as you can."

I chuckle, and Maisie looks at me, her eyes soft. "You look like you could use it the most."

"Should I take offense to that?" I tease, and she smirks,

shrugging. But before she can answer, I add, "I can make it in a minute. I know you're busy baking with Jake."

"No, please, let me do it," she insists gently. "It's the least I can do, all things considered."

Something passes between us—a quiet understanding—and once again, I want to reach for her. But instead, I tighten my grip on the wooden chair, resisting the urge.

"Okay, thanks," she says softly, turning to head back inside. I watch her go, then look back to find both Hayes and Luke grinning at me.

"Fuck off," I groan. "What are you doing here at the ass crack of dawn?"

"It's 0800, Flacco. Grow up."

"We wanted to check in—let you know what we found on our side."

"That doesn't sound good."

"Well—"

"OH MY GOD!"

I'm on my feet and sprinting inside before they can finish. Hayes and Luke are right behind me.

Inside, I find Maisie standing by the Miele with her phone in her hand.

"What?" I go to her instinctively.

"My... my... oh my god," she gasps, scrolling frantically.

Hayes groans, and I hear Luke curse behind me.

"What's happening?!" I demand, spinning Maisie to face me.

Tears fill her eyes, but she stays quiet and frozen.

Thankfully, Hayes breaks in. "The reviews?"

She nods, still trembling.

"What reviews?" I shoot a quick glance over my shoulder, keeping my grip firm on her shoulders.

"That's part of why we're here," Hayes explains.

"Stephanie created spam bots and littered Maisie's Google reviews with hundreds of negative comments."

"I'll handle it. I promise," I say, trying to get her to look at me, to believe that I'll move heaven and earth to fix this. And somehow, it works. She blinks away her tears and nods.

Without thinking, I wrap my arms around her, holding her close. "I'll get Jake set up with his Switch and the TV. I think it's probably best if you come out and hear the rest."

Before long, we're all sitting outside again, and my nerves are back on edge. My knee bounces at an all-time speed as I sit in the rocking chair, waiting to hear what else has happened.

They start unfolding everything—the break-in, the camera footage showing what appears to be a woman about Stephanie's height and weight breaking in, and the wreckage hitting Maisie's business with all the negative reviews. Lincoln has been working hard to keep her slander, the fake videos she posts, and the false claims from spreading across the internet. It's an onslaught—a deliberate attempt to destroy her livelihood, her sanity, and her reputation.

I see it on Maisie's face: the more they talk, the more frustration she feels, but at least she doesn't look sad anymore. She excuses herself to grab some muffins, and I brush her arm as she walks by. A small relief hits me when she doesn't pull away— she just offers a slight smile before going inside.

Suddenly, two phones start ringing at the same time— Hayes's and Luke's. They both look at each other, then at their phones.

Hayes answers his first. "Coop."

Luke answers his. "Lincoln."

Their expressions sharpen instantly. I catch a silent exchange—the news isn't good.

Luke's tone hardens as he relays, "I'll call Larkin." Bradley Larkin is the sheriff of the neighboring jurisdiction.

Hayes speaks low and measured, yet I hear the gravity in his voice, details that only someone trained would catch. My stomach knots as I observe the weight of their urgency. Meanwhile, I can hear Maisie inside chatting with Jake, explaining why muffins are the best breakfast food—an innocent moment amid chaos.

My skin feels itchy, overwhelmed by the barrage of information. I want to shield Jake, to protect Maisie, but I'm helpless. Luke steps away, already on another call, his movements tense. *Please let this nightmare end.* It's only Monday, yet it feels like days have passed since Saturday—since Jake was kidnapped. How has it taken Hayes's team so long? Hope flickers—if they've found her, she'll be in custody soon. That small victory hangs tantalizingly close yet seems so distant.

Rather than watch Luke and Hayes work outside, I slip inside, following the scent of freshly baked muffins and my girl's voice.

"I don't know what you made, but they smell amazing!" I say, leaning in the doorway.

Jake looks up, his face covered in chocolate, grinning widest of all. "DOUBLE chocolate!"

Maisie laughs, wiping her hands on her apron. "And the secret ingredient?"

"Zucchini! But, Dad, I swear, you can't even tell. They're so good."

Hayes comes in behind me, nose sniffing the air. "Chocolate muffins?"

"Double, Uncle Hayes. You gotta try one."

Luke pokes his head in, grabs a muffin, and ducks back outside to make his calls.

An hour or so later, Luke's phone rings again. He answers in that steady, official tone, shoulders tight with focus. Maisie tenses up on the couch; Jake's once again lost in his Mario game, oblivious. I look back, watching Luke bow his head briefly, almost in silent prayer, then he meets my eyes.

The words cut through the quiet like a shot: "We found her. She's in custody."

Relief slams into me—until Hayes's phone rings, and I overhear him talking to Lincoln, his shoulders stiff as steel.

When they both hang up, they exchange a tense glance.

"The guys think there's someone else involved."

"Larkin said it was only her in the house."

Hayes shrugs, voice low. "Call it a hunch."

My eyebrows pinch at the argument they are having, trying to understand the implications of what they are saying without actually saying.

"Come on, Hayes. You know I can't keep a detail team watching them based off a hunch."

He gives him a dry look. "Never asked you to. I trust my guys more than I trust yours, anyway."

Luke pauses, then nods slowly. "Yeah, me too, some days. Either way, it doesn't hurt to keep eyes on them until we're sure."

Hayes agrees with a serious nod. The tension is sharp but controlled—two sides with different approaches, united in the goal: keeping us safe.

The conversation may not have included me, but there aren't two men I trust more in life. They're the only thing that's kept me grounded during this situation, and Stephanie's been found—that's one worry I can check off for the day.

Chapter Twenty-One

Maisie

"Good morning girlies, it's the..." begins blaring through the radio of Ethan's truck as soon as he started it. *Is that?*

His hand scrambles to turn it off, but it's too late, the icon of Claudia and Jackie is on full display in front of me.

For the first time in years, I see a tinge of red hitting Ethan's cheeks, and his eyes are so wide that I can't help but giggle.

"*You* listen to 'The Toast?'"

"Dad listens to it in the mornings when he showers." Jake says from the back, and I turn to see him buckling his seat belt.

"You what?!" I try to control my laughter but simply can't.

He shrugs, "I told you I was borderline obsessed with you."

What does that mean? But rather than ask, my head rears back as I stare at him.

"You and Isla were talking about it at Ben's birthday party one year."

"So?"

"So I wanted to have something to talk to you about, if you ever gave me the chance."

"And you chose 'The Toast?!' Ethan! But..." My mind flashes back to all those very intimate, feminine conversations they've had over the years, and I can't help but laugh harder.

"Trust me, I skip through the girlie stuff... but, you know, some of it isn't *so* bad, *and* you can only listen to so much sports talk. It's a good break," he adds defensively.

"I—wow. I'm just... impressed? Although, that's a new low." And yet, I can't help but grin. He's always been a dork, but I can't even imagine him listening to a podcast just because he heard I liked it.

As we drive to Jake's t-ball game, the mood stays mostly light. Jake is on level ten, excited about his game and everyone that will be there to watch. I do my best to focus on Jake and ignore the side glances Ethan throughs my way. Ever since last night, it's like he's watching me through no longer rose-tinted glasses. Like he's waiting to pounce and ask the questions he's been wanting to for the last twelve years.

Even now, he glances at me from the driver's seat, his eyes flickering my way every so often, searching for something in my expression. I can practically hear the wheels turning in his mind, but at least he too is encouraging Jake, cheering him on for his last game of the season.

We arrive at the fields on a beautiful, sunny Central Oregon day; the warmth of June already enveloping us like a soft blanket. I take a moment to soak it in. The sun on my skin through the open window, the lush green fields stretching out before us, juxtaposed with the rugged land-scape of dirt and pine trees in the distance—it feels almost magical.

As we pass by Cooper's Durango, I spot Delta and Cooper standing beside it. "Hey!" I wave, feeling a flicker of warmth as they approach Ethan's truck.

Cooper leans in closer to the window with a smile that

makes his mustache tip up, but I can see him searching my face when he asks, "You doing okay?"

"Yeah, I'm alright," I reply, my smile becoming wider like he won't be able to see the cracks in it. "Just... one of those days, I guess." I propose, trying to play off yesterday like it was only a small thing.

I can feel the tension begin radiating off Ethan at my answer. It's subtle, but I notice it, the way his body tenses as if bracing for something.

"Not really sure if I believe that, Mais," Cooper says playfully, but I see the serious in his eyes. "But we got ya covered. Let us know if that changes."

"We'll be around," Delta replies with a nod, while Cooper slides to the back window and looks at Jake all smiles. "You ready to crush the Blue Lizards?"

Jake snorts in the back, "You know it, Coop!"

"Thanks, guys. Seriously," I say, grateful for their support. I know Ethan is paying them to keep a watch on everything going on, but that doesn't mean we aren't on all edge. Even with Stephanie being arrested, it all just felt too easy. So either she really is that dumb, or there's something we are missing.

After Ethan finds a parking spot, he leads Jake toward the dugout to start warming up, and I head over to the bleachers to sit by Olivia. She's perched next to Connie, Hayes's mom, who had practically become the only reliable mother of their entire group of misfits.

"Where's Drew?" I ask Olivia as I settle in, scanning the surroundings for familiar faces.

"Oh, he's one of the volunteer coaches," she replies, glancing towards the field. "But mostly, he hangs out with Ethan in the outfield and makes sure the kids know when and where to run."

Ben, who is a few rows ahead of us, engrossed in his

Nintendo Switch, sees a friend and immediately turns to his mom. I notice the worry flickering across Olivia's face when he yells, "Can we go to the playground?"

"Hey, I'll take them over there for a bit," Cooper offers, stepping in before Olivia can respond. She instantly relaxes, and I can see the burden lift from her shoulders. Even though the playground isn't far away, I can tell that having Cooper nearby eases her mind. It does the same for me if I'm being honest.

With the sun shining down and the sounds of children's laughter echoing around us, I try to focus on the joy of the moment. I'm here for Jake and Ellie, and I want to share in their excitement.

All that shifts the moment Levi arrives. He strolls over, exchanging friendly greetings with Drew, before leaning down to wish Jake and Ellie good luck. He's always been a good uncle to Ben and Ellie, and I've even seen him bring Jake into Maisie's on his days off. Everyone stepped up after we lost Dan, but Levi was there more than most—especially for Olivia and the kids.

That doesn't mean it didn't change him, though. I'm probably one of the few who can see how deep it runs. The mask he wears hides a sadness that never quite goes away—a pain he's learned to hide, even from himself. Kindred spirits and all that.

But he's also been there for me through the years. He's never forced me to talk about that night, and I've returned the favor—giving him the same courtesy. Still, I can see the toll it's taken—how stress has marked him, even if he tries to pretend otherwise.

I'd never call him out on it, though. Not because I don't see it, but because I respect his silence.

Then I notice Ethan nodding in Levi's direction, a subtle cue that sends a cold chill down my spine. They both walk away, away from where the kids are throwing to each other to warm up, but I can't catch what they're saying.

Olivia and Connie chatter on excitedly beside me, oblivious to the tension that seems to have suddenly filled the air. I try to focus on their conversation, but my mind keeps drifting back to Ethan and Levi's secretive exchange.

My stomach drops as I watch Ethan's dark expression as he strides back toward the dugout, his jaw set tight, tension radiating from his body as he eats up the space in long strides. And I'm not the only one to notice the shift; a quick glance at Drew, who looks between Ethan and Levi, confusion etched across his face as he watches Levi walk over to sit by Olivia.

"That can't be good." I murmur under my breath as the knot of worry forms in my gut.

By the way, Ethan looked ready to explode, I can't shake the feeling that Levi must have told him something, something that I should've told him long ago. The thought gnaws at me. *Would Levi throw me under the bus like that?* I can't foresee that happening, especially since he hasn't in the years before, but I also don't know what would have Ethan so riled up.

Every second spent watching Ethan storm toward the outfield feels like an eternity. I'm transfixed, watching the conflict brewing within him, the anger he's trying to contain. I've seen that look so many times—when a play doesn't go the way he thought it would, or when he feels like he's let his team down.

I take a deep breath, trying to center myself and squash the feelings stirring inside me. We are all here to watch Jake and Ellie and to cheer them on. Only, I'm having a hard time focusing, with Levi's leg bouncing a million miles a minute on the other side of Olivia—who's bending, twisting, and grumbling about the heat and the baby pushing on her bladder. There's the scowl on Ethan's face every time he looks over at us. Connie cheering at every play, whether it's for our team or the opponent. Cooper pretending to play with the kids at the playground, while Delta casually scans the entire area for threats. *It's all overwhelming.*

As soon as the game ends, I almost feel relief, that is, until Levi leans behind Olivia and looks at me with heartbreak on his face. "Hey, Maisie? Let's go for a drive." *Oh, shii-take mushrooms.*

Olivia's shoulders stiffen like she's been shocked, but she remains quiet, not even glancing between the two of us.

I nod, "Let me just tell the kids 'good game' and let Ethan know. And let the babysitters know. They'll probably have to follow..." I trail off, hoping he'll change his mind.

"All good. We aren't going far." Which means I have a pretty good guess of where he wants to go, and I'm not thrilled by it.

I know that it's time to have this conversation, know that I've been on borrowed time of repression, but that doesn't mean I was ready for it today. I don't know if I'll ever be ready for it, but after everything yesterday? I thought I had buried that part of myself and was moving on from my trauma. But now, I realize, I'm only ever a helping arm around my waist from spiraling again, the familiar panic rising in my chest, threatening to consume me whole. It's time to face the demons I've been avoiding for so long, no matter how much I wish I could keep them buried.

Chapter Twenty-Two

Maisie

"When'd ya get this?" I ask as I slide into Levi's new Ford pickup, the scent of fresh leather greeting me.

Ethan didn't say much when I told him I was getting a ride home with Levi and that I'd meet him at the house. He just gave me a long, sad look and nodded. Meanwhile, Jake was too excited about the after-T-ball party at the only pizza parlor in town to notice my absence.

"Two weeks or so ago," Levi replies with a heavy sigh, waiting for me to buckle my seatbelt before shifting into drive.

"That's nice…" I mumble, glancing back as Cooper's Durango pulls out behind us, the low rumble of their engines the only sound on the quiet road.

We ride in a weighty silence for a few minutes, and I try not to focus on the route he's taking. Deep down, I already know where we're headed. It isn't far from the fields, a ten-minute drive at most, but that knowledge does little to ease my nerves.

I've been out here countless times since it happened—driving past, stopping to stare at that random road he backed into. I've tried to make sense of it all, but have never been able to. It's been years, and I've done my best to repress those memories, to forget. But now, here we are, going to talk about it, with Cooper and Delta following closely behind. Thankfully, they're unaware of what happened, though they're perceptive enough to sense there's more going on. I just hope I can hold it together long enough to get through this conversation and finally put that chapter of my life to rest.

When Levi slows down and signals, I realize I'm shaking like a Chihuahua in a snowstorm. He parks in the same spot he did that night, and we both stare at the dirt road, as if the ghosts are still lurking, haunting us. Silence hangs between us for a few minutes, but it gives me a chance to calm down, to regulate my breathing and gather my thoughts.

This is just a location in the world, coordinates on a map; it doesn't hold power over me. The memories won't define me. The past has no bearing on who I am today.

"Her name was Sienna. We'd been hanging out for a little while. Met on campus after class one day—things progressed pretty quickly, actually. But then—" His voice cracks, and I can hear the raw emotion behind his words, yet he sounds distant as he recounts Sienna and their time in college. "She died."

"What? How? When?" I gasp, suddenly aware I'd never asked about her until now.

"Pulmonary embolism, I guess? Her family didn't tell me much. They weren't exactly thrilled about me hanging around her. It was, I don't know, a month or so after that night."

"Levi—I'm so—"

He cuts me off, his eyes fixed on the darkened road ahead. "I know. I didn't bring you out here to unpack my shit though. It's just relevant to why I am the way I am, you know? Sienna, if she hadn't been there... I wouldn't have stopped." His pain is unmistakable, and I realize just how deeply he's been affected by that night. The unknown weight he has been carrying of nearly killing someone.

"And if you hadn't been there, he wouldn't have... stopped." I reach out and place my hand on his arm, still holding the steering wheel, giving it a gentle squeeze before retreating it.

"No, he wouldn't have," he agrees, his expression somber, but a dark chuckle comes from him. "Kept tabs on him after that—well, dad did."

I gasp with horror and on an exhale demand, "your dad knows?"

"Yeah, Maisie. I had to tell him. Scottie could barely fucking walk after. Had to push back going to boot camp for four weeks because of what I did to him."

"I didn't—I didn't know that."

"Well, we never really talked about it, beyond those times when I'd find you curled up, having a panic attack. Thought those were gone, by the way?"

"They are—were, I guess. I was already losing it over my apartment being ransacked, and then Leo thought he was being helpful and put his arm around me."

He nods, a look of understanding crossing his face. "After Margie picked you up that night, Sienna and I drove him to the hospital. Her mom worked there as a nurse, and I think, in hindsight, that was the night she decided not to like me. Anyway, I called my dad and his parents. You were adamant about not wanting anyone to know what happened, but I couldn't just let it go without telling someone. Scottie was in pretty bad shape, and I needed help figuring out what to do next. My dad and his parents had it out for sure, but Scottie eventually admitted he crossed a line while helping a friend with a ride home and that he could see why I'd think more was goin' on."

"Your dad let it go?" I ask, disbelief creeping into my voice.

Zeke was never known for being a lenient sheriff; I can't wrap my head around the fact that he wasn't on my parents' doorstep the very next day, demanding a statement.

"On the condition that he left town and never came back. His parents ended up moving back to Montana, too," Levi replies, his gaze fixed on the road ahead, the grip on the steering wheel tightening slightly.

"I heard that, but it was just town gossip that he got a job back there," I say, crossing my arms tightly over my chest, trying to ward off the unease settling in.

"I think they were afraid you might eventually come forward. Doesn't look good for the new pastor in town's son to be accused of attempted rape."

I wince at his words, the truth stinging, but I know he's right.

"Do you know where he ended up? I haven't heard anything about him since he left," I continue, my voice barely above a whisper.

"Dead," Levi states bluntly, glancing at me before returning his focus to the front window. "He got a dishonorable discharge a few years after he enlisted. I don't know the details, but reportedly, he ended up on a fishing boat in Alaska. Then he went overboard—or was thrown," he adds, his tone casual, as if he's talking about the weather.

I turned to stare at him, my eyes widening in shock. He merely shrugs, an unsettling calm radiating from him. "He was a bad fucking dude. Piss off the wrong person out there? Surprised they even found his body."

A chill runs down my spine, and I shift in my seat, feeling the weight of his words settle between us, heavy and unshakeable. The thought of him meeting such a tragic end doesn't surprise me, but it also doesn't bring me any comfort. That night lingers in the back of my mind, gnawing at me.

We fall into a heavy silence, processing everything from the attack to Levi finding me lying on the floor at the Coffee Hut, back when it wasn't Maisie's yet. I remember it vividly; it was just a few weeks after the attack when Leilani had been the customer before Levi, talking about how great the bonfire had been. I held it together as she rambled on, but when she drove away, flashbacks to leaving in that truck flooded my mind, and then it all went dark. Levi literally jumped through the drive-thru window and talked me through it. He wasn't even officially a paramedic, but he knew exactly what to do.

After that, he stuck around, checking in often and sending me articles he found on panic attacks and breathing exercises. He even offered to go to therapy with me, even though I always declined.

The thought hits me as quick as the sob following does—he found me just a few weeks after the attack, which must have been right around the time Sienna died.

"Levi—" I choke out, the tears streaming down my face.

Startled, he turns in his seat, fully facing me, his bright blue eyes immediately looking panicked. "What?"

"How long after she died did you start helping me?"

His hand that was extending toward me unconsciously falls midway, and his eyes grow distant. "Right after," he admits quietly. "I had just left the hospital and was driving home. I was mostly in a daze—and then I saw Leilani pulling away and you just... fell." His vulnerability catches me off guard, and I can see the pain in his eyes as he recounts the moment.

"I had no idea. I should've—" Should've known. Should've been helping him. Should've been more aware of his pain. "I'm so sorry I wasn't there for you like you were there for me."

"You may not have known what happened, but you helped me through it. All those articles I was sending you? They weren't just for you."

"Okay…" I reply, still not convinced.

"Do you know what I regret about this situation? It's not kicking Scottie's ass or anything with Sienna. What I regret is letting you handle it your way and wasting all this time away from Ethan."

"That wasn't for you to decide," I shoot back.

"No, it wasn't. But you should have told him."

"He wouldn't be where he is today if I had!" I defend myself, frustration creeping into my tone.

"You don't know that, Maisie!" he snaps, raising his voice. "You don't know how he would've handled it or how he'll handle it now. I feel like *I've* been lying to him for so long, and I can't keep doing that. I won't keep doing that. I know what it's like to be shut out of something important."

He leans in closer, his eyes piercing. "*You* need to tell him the truth. He deserves to know. All of it."

"He's going to look at me differently—like I should have known better," I say, my voice trembling.

"Maybe. Or maybe he'll finally understand why you kept it from him. Either way, he deserves the truth and the chance to decide how to feel about it."

"Levi, I don't know if I can," I admit, feeling the weight of it all pressing down on my heart.

"The only thing keeping you from letting it go, from truly moving forward, is this secret. It's got you bound up, forever tied to this place," he says, pointing toward the dirt road. "The world has moved on and forgotten about the injustice that happened here. Scottie is dead—not through any fault of his own—but you're still alive, carrying this burden? Let it go, Maisie. Don't die with this secret still inside you. Not when you have someone who loves you right in front of you, begging to help you release it. That man has proved time and time again that he loves you. Let him."

I take a deep breath, feeling the truth of his words sink in.

I turn to face him, tears welling in my eyes as I finally begin to release the weight I've been carrying for so long. "Take me to Ethan," I whisper.

"Take me home." And I'm not sure how in only forty-eight hours his house has become my house, but somehow that's what it is. Maybe because he built it for me, maybe because it was always meant to be, but it's home.

Chapter Twenty-Three

Ethan

Maisie's already home by the time I pull down the drive, and I spot Cooper's SUV parked in the driveway. Jake had asked to sleep over at Olivia's house, and I couldn't have agreed faster. After my attempt at a heart-to-heart with Levi, where he told me absolutely nothing, I'm more determined than ever to talk to Maisie.

As I walk into the house, the smell of chocolate chip cookies fill the air. Maisie baking is either a good sign or a very, very bad one.

I nod hello to the guys, who are sitting in the formal living room, but they both quickly shift their eyes away from me.

"You good for us to head out?" Delta asks, and I swear he looks exhausted.

"Yeah, thanks. Everything—?" I start to ask, but I'm cut off when Maisie steps out of the kitchen. She's wearing an apron over the sundress she had on earlier, and she takes my breath away as she carries a plate of cookies.

"You're here!" she squeaks, and I can't help but smile. "Wow, okay. Wow. Uhm, here ya go, guys. Thanks for... you know, making sure I don't get unalived." She sets the cookies down, shoots them an awkward smile, and then retreats back to the kitchen.

I glance at the guys, confused, and they both shrug in response. Cooper grabs the entire plate, saying, "We'll get out of here." He still doesn't make eye contact, which only makes me want to hit them and then demand to know what's going on.

Delta walks next to me, and I level him with a look. His hands go up defensively as he whispers the unspoken message —"Hour and a half parked on 242, near a forest service road." I instantly recognize the general area he's referring to. We used to take that highway to go deeper into the forest for bonfires and parties, and that was the route everyone took to get home. "Just talked, man. But... something must have happened there."

I can only nod in response. *Something happened there— something that changed the course of my life forever.* I had a feeling their ride was meant for this conversation, and I also sense that Levi chose a side. My hope is that it's mine—that he convinced her to tell me what happened.

The guys leave, and finally, we are alone.

I walk into the kitchen with heavy feet and an anxious heart, hoping today is the day she opens up, but I'm also terrified of what I might hear.

The more I've thought about it, the more I realize whatever it is must have been so traumatic that she wouldn't share it with me.

She's sitting at the counter, the spot she's occupied for the last three breakfasts, which I now think of as her spot.

As she spins on her chair to face me, I see the first tear roll down her cheek.

I start to approach her, but she holds up a hand. "If you come over here and touch me, I'll break down and won't be able to get through this."

I plant my feet firmly on the tile, waiting for her to go on. "I need to get this all out, and I need you to save your questions and comments until after."

"Okay," she continues, taking a deep breath. "After the grad party, Olivia and I went to the after-party bonfire." I nod, but I stay quiet; I've known she went to the bonfire and went home early.

"We were just hanging out, talking to everyone. But then it got overwhelming, and I was exhausted. I just wanted to go home."

Why were you overwhelmed? The question lingers in my mind but goes unvoiced.

"Scottie—do you remember him? He offered to give me a ride back to town to my car."

I blink at her; of course, I remember Scottie. The guy was an asshole with a chip on his shoulder, always trying to mess with me and the team. The things he said in the locker room were beyond that of normal guy talk.

"He hadn't been drinking, and Leilani wanted to keep talking to Brandon, so I agreed..."

"On the way home, I just had this weird feeling," she begins, her voice trembling. "But I ignored it. Then he... he pulled over, off to the side of the road, and backed down a side road. I didn't understand why."

She pauses, her breath coming in shaky pants that echo the trembling I feel deep in my chest. A heavy weight presses on me, like I've known the truth all along but couldn't bring myself to accept it.

"He said something was wrong with the engine or something. I got out to help him hold the light, and then he... he..." Her voice falters, and my stomach tightens, my head spinning, waiting for her to say it—the words I dread most, the confirmation of something terrible happening to her that night. I cling to the silence, bracing myself for the blow.

"I tried at first," she whispers, voice barely audible, "but then I just... I froze." The vulnerability in her voice stabs me worse than rage ever could.

"Levi got there in time," she blurts out, her voice suddenly steadier, though haunted. "He saved me. Scottie's dead." *Levi killed Scottie for Maisie...*

The words hit like a punch to the gut. I must look stunned, because she quickly hurriedly adds, "Levi didn't kill him. He died on a fishing boat. Levi just put him in the hospital... but no one else knows that. Well, Zeke does. And Scottie's family. But it was all hush-hush. I didn't even find out until Levi told me today. Zeke banned him from town, and he listened. His parents left too."

I nod slowly, trying to process everything, but inside, a wildfire is burning—hot, uncontrollable. My mind spins with fury and helplessness. My fists clench so tightly that I feel every bone tense up.

Then she takes a deep breath, steadying herself. "And then..." she whispers softly, her voice trembling again, her eyes searching mine.

Once again, I feel as if I've been pulled underwater— drowning in all the truth I've spent twelve years desperately trying to hear.

"And then I started having panic attacks," she continues, voice raw. "A lot of them. Right around the time the girl who went with Levi to the party that night died." She pauses, then adds with a somber tone, "Sorry, I didn't mention her. Sienna. Her name was Sienna. Levi was kind of with her or something. She was the one who pulled Levi off Scottie before he could kill him."

Sienna—Levi's dead girlfriend. She saved Scottie. But she

died after Maisie was attacked—and before Scottie died in that fishing accident. My head reels, trying to make sense of everything.

"So the panic attacks started after Sienna died," she says quietly, "and Levi began mentoring me on how to deal with the anxiety."

She hesitates, her voice softening. "I guess he was having some issues too, but I didn't know that at the time. I also started going to therapy, thanks to Margie's insistence. It helped a lot, actually. But I stopped going after—" Her voice trails off, and she wrings her hands in her lap, avoiding my gaze.

"Why didn't you tell me? When it happened? Why push me away? I would have—"

"Dropped everything to help me? Ruined your career? How could you have left just a few days later and focused on anything other than me and what happened?"

She continues, her voice trembling. "It wasn't just that, though. I felt... dumb and dirty, like it was my fault. I shouldn't have gone and put myself in that position. I was mad you left with Alexandra and wanted to prove to myself that I could still be a person after you were gone, but then I stopped trusting myself. It took me a long time to understand why I reacted the way I did—why I froze. Therapy helped with that part, but it was all the other stuff swirling around in my head that weighed me down, and... you were doing so well, Ethan. You were truly living up to your potential, becoming one of the greats."

"Why not come to me after I got back?"

"Because of the way you're looking at me right now. I'm not your fierce Maisie anymore. I froze."

I step closer, my hands resting gently on the counter behind her—careful not to touch her.

"That's not— that's not how I see you, Maisie. Hell, you quite literally saved my son a few days ago. You don't know if you would have fought back after that. You froze, and then Levi was there. You might have been the one to kill him. We don't know, but I'd never think of you as anything less than strong."

And then she kisses me.

The kiss is tentative at first—a soft brush of lips that sparks something deep inside me, igniting all my senses. I feel her hesitate briefly, but then her lips deepen the kiss, and my heart races. In that instant, all the pain, all the misunderstandings, and the distance between us seem to melt away.

As I pull back slightly, searching her eyes for reassurance, her breath comes in soft gasps. "Ethan..." she whispers, a plea and a question wrapped in one.

"It can wait," I murmur, closing the distance again, enveloping her in the warmth of my embrace. My hands find her waist, pulling her closer, as if I need to fuse our bodies together—make this moment last forever.

The world outside fades away, and it's just us in that kitchen, but even with the lingering shadows of our past, everything feels electric. I guide her gently back, my hands moving up to cradle her face, our lips brushing softly, urgently.

I take a step back, holding her gaze. "Come on," I say softly, leading her away from the kitchen, the warmth of the cookies long forgotten. I sense her heart racing as I take her hand, walking her down the dimly lit hall toward the bedroom.

With each step, I can feel the tension in the air shift—this place that once held so many memories of hurt is now charged with a different kind of energy. I pause at the door, my pulse racing, and glance back to see a flicker of uncertainty in her eyes.

"You okay with this?" I ask, my voice low and steady.

She nods, a small yet resolute smile breaking through her lingering apprehension. "Yeah, I want this."

I push the door open and step inside, the soft glow of the

bedside lamp casting shadows on the walls. It's a space that feels like home, yet tonight it transforms into a sanctuary just for us.

As I turn back to her, I reach out, tucking a strand of hair behind her ear before pulling her into me again. Our lips meet once more, igniting a fire within as I guide her toward the bed. I can feel her body responding instinctively—soft, warm, inviting.

As we collapse onto the bed, bodies entwined and breaths mingling, it feels like everything around us fades into oblivion. The chaos, the pain, the unspoken words—it all falls away, leaving just us in this moment, ready to embrace whatever comes next.

Chapter Twenty-Four

Maisie

"So... you really built me this house, bought the Miele, *and* listen to quite possibly the girliest podcast out there—all because you thought I'd like it?" I ask as the sun starts to light up the sky behind us, creating dark blue skies on the fields beyond us. Neither of us got more than a few blinks of sleep last night, and somehow ended up on the back patio, wrapped in a cozy blanket.

His hand delicately traces my bare leg as it rests over his lap. The relief I feel after confessing everything is insurmountable, even though I know it was just the first conversation of many. The way he let me talk, get it all out there, and controlled his emotions so that I could throw mine out there, was undoubtedly what I needed.

"Maisie, if anyone knew the things I did to still feel close to you, I'd be arrested for stalking."

"You can't joke about that stuff, here!"

His laugh rumbles in his chest, "I wasn't buying roses, but I was listening for your name in every conversation. Paying for my employees' coffees just so they'd bring me one of your cookies. Hell, Callie uses the company card anytime she goes in and brings me something for every shift."

"Ethan!" I admonish, smacking his chest.

"Maisie, I never gave up hope. Not once," he says, voice steady but full of meaning. "There were times I was more obsessed than others, but I would've waited a lifetime for you."

I look down, swallowing hard. "I know it doesn't make sense to say I would've too, but I wasn't dating anyone either. Couldn't, without it feeling like I was doing something wrong. Leo didn't even ask me out—it was Cooper implying I should, and I nearly threw up after I said yes."

He exhales softly, like he's fighting back everything he's holding inside. "Can you believe that was, what, five days ago? Odessa comes into Ponderosa and tells me Leo's taking you on a date, and I almost lost it. Even then, it felt like the catalyst."

His voice tightens. "But if you knew the spiral I was in at the line for the rodeo? Pfft. You just walked up and started talking to Jake, and I swear I blacked out from nerves. Somehow, in that moment, the line you drew in the sand was being washed away. I didn't know if it was because of Leo, or what. And then everything with Jake—I was about to lose my goddamn mind."

He pauses, voice thick with emotion. "Until... until I saw you in that car with him. Fuck, Maisie. I just knew. I knew we weren't going back to not talking. I wasn't going to let you get away again. And as much as I *fucking* hate Stephanie, she changed it all for us. That made the worst six hours of my life worth every second of pain."

I swallow hard, feeling every word hit me to the core. "It only took a kidnapping, a gun to my head, and a panic attack— to realize that the fear I'd been holding onto was keeping me paralyzed to that night. But yeah—without all that, I'd probably still be ignoring you, obsessing over you too."

He lets out a soft, rough laugh. "Had I known you were best friends with my kid, I might have used him to my advantage a long time ago."

I smile, a little breathless. "He's the best. I actually looked forward to seeing him on Fridays. And I always wondered—what if you'd answered that phone all those years ago? Maybe everything would've been so different. But then, Jake wouldn't be here. I guess, with everything that's happened, I'm starting to accept that maybe everything does happen for a reason."

He stares at me, silent for a beat. Then, quietly, he asks, "What phone call?"

I clear my throat, feeling suddenly nervous. "I, um, I actually tried to call you a few nights after the championship game your freshman year. My therapist thought it would be a good way to bridge the gap."

"What do you mean, you tried?"

I stutter a bit, sensing the intensity in his voice. "It—Um, well, I—"

"Mais, spit it out," he urges, his voice raw and whisper-like.

"Alexandra answered the phone."

"Alexandra? Why would she answer my phone?" he asks, as if I haven't wondered the same question every day since it happened. "Oh, shit. The Frenches were in town that weekend, and she ended up staying a few days longer."

I shrug, remaining silent. I can see him deep in thought, trying to remember a time so long ago. I can't help but wonder if they still talk. I haven't heard Winnie mention them in a while, but I know they still travel to see them during the summer.

"She never said anything. What did she say?"

"She said..." I pause, recalling her words, and my stomach turns all over again. "Let's just say she was very defensive of you and the things that happened between us."

"What exactly did she say, Maisie?"

"It's been a long time, Ethan. I don't remember the exact words." I can almost hear her voice in my head: "You're an absolute worthless human being for leading Ethan on like that and then leaving him high and dry. He's been a wreck since you stopped talking to him, and the fact that you think it's okay to call after everything you've done is despicable. He deserves better than you, and we both know it."

"She didn't know what happened, though, and she was right—I had cut you off recklessly... but that conversation sent me spiraling. I ended up stopping therapy and tried to focus on school and baking instead, which actually turned out to be good because I was super prepared for Maisie's when I finally had the chance to start it."

"Good? Come on, Mais." He runs his hands through his hair in frustration. "Fuck, I can't even say that. It's not fair. Jake is good. I wouldn't change that, but knowing you called, that you tried, and it ended up hurting you more? That's—all of it— it's fucked up."

We sit in silence for a moment, letting our feelings settle, before he sighs heavily.

I reach over, grabbing his chin and turning it toward me. The rawness in his eyes could be earth-shattering, so much so it brings tears to me eyes. "Everything happens for a reason. If that reason is so that Jake is on this earth, so be it. I'll take the years of pain for this," I gesture toward the fields, "because this moment is worth all the bad moments. To have you back? After I thought I could never have you? My eighteen-year-old heart is healing and doing backflips."

His eyes soften as he mouths, "Mine too."

"I love you and I love Jake," I whisper, feeling the weight of it in my chest.

Before I can fully register it, he leans in and kisses me

again. His lips are warm, and I can feel the happiness radiating from him — like a quiet, steady pulse.

"I love you too," he affirms.

We stay like that for a moment, bathed in the quiet comfort of each other, until he finally breaks the silence with a gentle nudge.

"So, what's going on this week? Any big things at Maisie's that'll have you busy?"

I chuckle softly, the mood shifting to something lighter.

"Not so much at Maisie's. Drew asked me to bake Olivia some birthday cupcakes—wants to get them early, just in case she goes into labor," I explain.

He lights up quickly. "You should use the kitchen here! Jake and I can be your taste testers."

I smile at that—his enthusiasm is contagious. "I'd love that."

He tilts his head with a grin. "Oh, and while we're at it, what do you think about having a BBQ this weekend? We can celebrate the end of the school year—and maybe her early birthday, too."

My eyebrows raise in playful challenge. "Fun! But you know that means you have to let me help."

He shakes his head, smirking. "Nah, I don't want you lifting a finger. We'll have the restaurant cater it."

I lift an eyebrow, giving him a sly look. "You're a dream come true, Flacco."

"Same for you, My Perfect Maisie."

Chapter Twenty-Five

Maisie

Jake and I spent the rest of yesterday baking three dozen cupcakes, and they turned out pretty darn good. We made chocolate chai cupcakes—moist, rich, and full of warm chai spice notes. I plan to top them with a lightly sweet whipped cream cheese frosting infused with fresh blackberry purée. I know Olivia's favorite drink is a dirty chai, so I wanted to make something a little different and special just for her.

I still plan to do most of the decorating myself today, but having Jake's help was a nice break. Ethan picked him up from school and took him over to his parents' house, knowing Winnie's still pretty shaken up after everything with the kidnapping. I get why Ethan's been trying to keep Jake close to her—Winnie's fragile right now, and they both need time to heal. Plus, I asked if it would be okay to invite my parents over tonight to "talk." He understood immediately and told me he was proud of me for taking that step.

But now, I'm left in this big, quiet house. Liam's in the library, doing who knows what, but he's so quiet I keep forgetting he's even here. I made him a sandwich for lunch earlier, and I got one beautiful sentence out of him—the rarest of victories. He took a bite and said, "It's amazing—Thank you, Maisie."

I left the office feeling pretty proud of myself. That was hours ago, and since then, I've done nothing but twiddle my thumbs until it was time to start prepping the frosting.

While I heated the blackberries in a saucepan with a splash of water, my mind started to drift—thinking about how tonight might go. I'd invited my parents for dinner, maybe to try a cupcake, but mostly, it was a ruse to tell them everything about graduation night—the whole crazy, terrifying story. My therapist had thought it was a good idea back when I still saw her, but I'd never quite had the courage. That was, until this morning, when I finally convinced myself, I did. I told Ethan—that should've been the hardest part.

So why is my skin suddenly prickling with heat? Why is my chest tightening?

I continue to watch the mixer whirl—the blackberries swirling into the frosting—while my vision blurs slightly around the edges. A rush of dizziness washes over me, and I become acutely aware of how uneven my breathing has become. Thump. Thump. Thump. My pulse pounds louder in my ears, blending with the noise from the mixer, and suddenly, it feels like I'm drowning.

Focus. I clutch at the countertop, trying to ground myself, but my hands tremble. My head spins, nausea rolling around in my stomach, and I squeeze my eyes shut for a second, willing the wave to pass. I just want to breathe normally again—just breathe.

Then, like a reflex, my brain screams: *Call Margie!*

I reach for my phone, fumbling to tap her name—

"What's up, sis?" Margie's voice crackles through.

"I did something... I invited mom and dad over," I admit, my voice tense and nearly out of the breath.

"Okay?" I hear chaos in the background—clattering, kids yelling—the sort of noise that's not exactly conducive to my rising anxiety.

"Margie! Can you go somewhere quiet for two minutes while I freak out?" I plead.

"Everyone listen—if you can be quiet for ten minutes, Maisie will bring you Rice-Krispie treats this weekend," she offers, a hint of humor in her voice.

"Oh, thanks," I grumble, feeling absurd.

"Sorry, bribery's the only way sometimes. Plus, see? They're quiet," she says, trying to lighten the mood.

"Why is it so crazy there right now?" I ask, my body already starting to relax by the distraction.

"Ugh," she huffs. "Jason's been gone for days, working late on some project. I dunno, I think the kids are rebelling and really testing me."

"It is what it is," she continues. "So, what's got you freaking out?"

"I invited mom and dad over, and they should be here any minute. I'm going to tell them about—"

Suddenly, I get cut off by the chime alert—someone's going through the gate.

"Shit, they're here."

"Maisie, it's okay. They—"

"I know, I know. It'll be fine. Love you!" I hang up and quickly get back to work, stuffing the frosting into piping bags. My heart's still pounding in my chest, but talking to Margie has helped calm some of the nerves.

"Hello!" There's no knocking—just the door swinging open as they stroll in and a shouted greeting. That's pretty typical when they come to my apartment, but it still surprises me, especially since this is Ethan's house.

"In the kitchen!"

And then I remember—how they've always stayed close to Ethan, even despite my falling out with him. They've never mentioned it, never made a fuss. Margie would casually mention my mom dropping off eggs for Ethan here and there, or I'd catch my dad talking to Ethan about a game. It's like they've tried to keep that connection alive—even if I cut myself off completely.

And now that I'm thinking about it... shouldn't they have wondered why I refused to talk to him?

"Maisie Paisie," my mom greets with a wide grin, pulling me into a hug before glancing at the dozens of cupcakes sitting out.

My dad steps closer, his eyes flicking over the cupcakes before settling on me with that familiar, knowing look.

"I'm surprised you're still staying here," he says with a gentle tease. "Given the kitchen, maybe I shouldn't be, though."

I let out a nervous laugh, feeling the mess of nerves kicking in. "Well... I'd like to talk to you about that," I admit quietly, my voice lowering.

My dad exchanges a quick glance with my mom, who's all smiles but has that slightly tense look behind her eyes. She grins wider, as if she already knows what's coming.

"But there's actually something else I want to talk about first," I say softly, carefully picking up the piping bag, already gearing up for the next step of the peony design. I line up the cupcake and prepare to start piping the petals—this is one of those designs I've practiced a hundred times. I could do it in my sleep.

Yet, even with my attention fixed on the delicate work, I

keep my focus sharp. Each arc of icing comes out steady and perfect—I can do this in my sleep.

"I never really explained why I stopped talking to Ethan," I finally said, my voice steady but quiet enough that I could hear my heartbeat pounding in my ears.

They stayed silent, and I could feel the weight of the room's thick silence pressing down on me. The energy shifted—tense, crackling—and I kept going.

"Graduation night... something happened. It changed everything," I whispered, squeezing the icing bag gently to keep the flow smooth. The petals I was piping looked flawless—like I'd planned.

"You don't have to explain if it's too hard, honey. We know," my mom said softly.

"You know?!" I nearly dropped the icing bag, my hand trembling slightly, but I forced my grip to stay steady. I didn't dare look up, my throat tight, trying to swallow down the pain.

My dad finally broke the silence, voice gentle but sure. "We know."

"Margie?" I asked, my voice trembling with disbelief, almost afraid to say it out loud.

"No," my mom said at the same time my dad replied, "Zeke."

That's when I finally looked up. Both of them looked guilty —at least, they looked caught, red-handed. I saw tears glistening in my mom's eyes, but she was quick to wipe them away. My dad sighed heavily, rubbing the back of his neck, as if trying to push away whatever guilt he was carrying.

"Zeke?" I whispered, my voice cracking. "He... told you?"

"We've been waiting until you approached us to have this conversation. But yeah, honey, we've known since the morning after it all happened."

"Zeke showed up on our doorstep. You were locked away in

your room, and we just assumed you'd had a late night and were still sleeping."

"I—well, yes, but I didn't know he was there," I said, voice trembling.

"He wanted to make sure you didn't want to press charges. Margie came down while he was there. She explained everything from your side, and we all agreed that the second you were ready to talk, we'd take you there. She promised us she'd get you into therapy."

"If he hadn't explained how close Levi was to killing him, I'm not sure I wouldn't have killed him myself," my dad admits, tears glistening in his eyes. Something I've rarely seen before—he's always been the strong one.

The images of Levi and a bloody Scottie flash through my mind, and I feel a sob raking through my body. Levi really risked everything that night, and I don't think I ever truly understood the gravity of it until now.

"We didn't want to drop it," he continues, "but we also wanted to respect your wishes to Marg. She said you didn't want the town knowing, didn't want them thinking of you differently." She grows quiet, the emotion thickening her voice when she asks, "Was that the right choice? We've struggled for years over that decision. Especially with your refusal to talk to Ethan."

"No, Mom," I say quickly. "That's exactly what I would've wanted you to do. And even though it was justified, it wouldn't have looked good for Levi."

She hesitates, then softly adds, "I'm sorry we didn't tell you we knew. You just pretended like it was nothing for so long, we never knew how to talk to you about it. I don't want you to think we didn't care—"

"No, Mom," I cut her off. "I get it. I didn't want to talk about it, either. It would've been so much harder if I'd known you knew. Truthfully, it's kind of a relief to know you knew but still treated me the same. That was one of the things I was so worried about."

She reaches out, her voice gentle. "We'd never think of you any differently. Levi... well, he's an honorary member of the family."

"Yeah... He really was there for me, after everything," I say softly.

Then my mom asks hesitantly, "So, Ethan knows now?" I nod.

My dad grunts more than speaks, "You movin' in here?"

I hesitate. "I—if he'll let me..."

"Pfft. If he'll let you? He'll have you moved in within an hour of you telling him," he says confidently, a broad grin spreading across his face.

I smile back and look at my dad. He's smiling too.

"You're okay with that?"

"Without a doubt."

And that final blessing is all I need—I'm moving into my house.

Chapter Twenty-Six

Ethan

I pull into the parking lot of Ponderosa Pine, feeling the weight of the past two weeks bearing down on me, even though Callie's been doing an amazing job holding things together. As I step inside, I spot her behind the bar, chatting with some of the staff. She's a pint-sized ball of energy, with blonde hair and bangs that highlight her bright blue eyes, giving her an instantly cheerful and mischievous look. If one more of my customers says she looks like Sabrina Carpenter, I may lose my mind.

With a wave, I motion for her to follow me to my, well our, office.

Tossing my keys and mail onto the desk, I then sit down and wait for Callie. My head naturally falls back, closing my eyes while it rests on the back of the chair. I can already feel a headache coming on, and the desire to get out of here pulsing through me. Not that I have anywhere to be, Jake's at school doing his "field-day" events for the last week and Maisie is at work, where Cooper is watching over her. I know because I cruised through on my way here for a pastry and a good morning kiss. A lot has changed, but she's still up at the crack of dawn and heading into work like she wasn't just in an all out fist fight, had a severe panic attack, and then revealed quite possibly the biggest secret Three Sisters has ever had.

"Hey, boss man." Callie greets me with a knock on the door.

"Hey, how are things holding up," I say without looking up at her.

"Things are good. We've been steady, a lot of people coming in and out. Some looking for the story, but mainly the regulars and tourists passing through." I'd already known that the kidnapping attempt had hit the press, and then with Stephanie's arrest, I knew things would get heated. Surprisingly, it's stayed pretty quiet, though. The town has mostly rallied together and decided that any press is bad press, and they don't want anyone sniffing around. They may gossip together, but outsiders will have a tough time getting a story after everything that's happened in the last year.

Sitting up, I nod, "Had a feeling that would be the case. Think Lincoln's been doing some media control as well to keep things at bay."

"What did we ever do without those guys?" she asks with a heavy sigh and dreamy eyes.

I shrug and can't help but grumble, "pretty sure they brought quite a bit of drama themselves."

"Yeah," she says, lowering her voice a tad, "so, is everything okay? I know they have Stephanie, but the gossip throughout town is that they don't think she was working alone."

I lean on the desk, feeling depleted again. "This needs to stay in this office, between us... but no, the guys don't think she was working alone. They still don't have proof, but they're trying to figure it out."

Callie curses under her breath, but looks at me sympathetically. "I assume you still have the Bod Squad watching Maisie and Jake?"

I scrunch my nose at the nickname the girls gave Hayes and Drews' team but nod. "Yeah, they're rotating shifts for now."

"Good. They'll keep them both safe. On to the next order of business, and unfortunately, it kind of involves Maisie." My head tilts, curious about where she's going with this.

"Jason was in again last night, too drunk and making a scene." *Shit.* Maisie's brother-in-law has a habit of making an ass of himself lately, and I hate being the bad guy, but in this industry, it can be necessary.

"What happened?" I ask with a heavy sigh.

"Not much, thankfully. I was covering for Kade when he came stumbling in, so I handled it. Wherever he was before must have kicked him out because he was toasted when he walked in. I didn't serve him anything other than fries and water—which really pissed him off—but he was a liability."

"Good," I nod, confirming. "I appreciate that. I would've done the same."

She clears her throat. "I texted Margie, too. Let her know he was in rough condition. But—"

"But?"

"I don't know. Don't take this the wrong way, and it's definitely not my business... but I think she's checked out. Or fed up? Used to it?"

I nod but stay quiet, waiting for her to keep going.

"Maybe you could just watch out for her? I don't know, something's telling me there's more going on, and she's turning a blind eye—maybe not a blind eye, but avoiding it because she can't handle anything else?"

"I can do that. I'll check in with Maisie and see if she's noticed anything." Maisie's always stayed close with Margie, but I can't recall a time I've seen her hanging out with Jason—

and for someone who is Maisie borderline obsessive, you'd think I'd have noticed. Jason's always been an odd one, though. I wouldn't say I'm close with him, but we shoot the shit about football periodically. He was also the one that I hired to paint our house. Then again, that was when I first moved home and was doing whatever I could to get in Maisie's good graces.

"Thanks—sorry to get you involved. I know things are still rocky over there, but I don't want Margie to get caught up in something because Jason's a drunk fool."

We pause for a moment, both of us reflecting quietly, the weight of the conversation settling between us.

"Anyway, on to the next. The beginning of summer barbecue you're hosting? I know you'll have Chef Julian cater it, but what else do you need?"

"Thinking a bartender who either wants to set up the food or a server willing to come help."

"What about CJ? He can handle that easily, and I think he's ready for some hands-on bartending training. He's been really great the last few weeks."

"I like that. See if he's up for it. Any chance you want to help out too? I'm happy to pay double if you think he could use the guidance—unless, of course, you just want to come hang out and celebrate."

She extends her hand over her chest, smirking. "Appreciate the offer, but no 'hanging out' for me. I need the money, and I need to be careful with drinking around those guys, so I don't end up with a broken heart or pregnant," she winks.

"Ha. Ha. Very funny."

Footsteps sound from down the hall, and CJ walks by, balancing a box of produce in his arms, heading toward Chef Julian's prep station. Callie hollers out, "Hey, CJ! Boss man's throwing a barbecue at his place this weekend. Want to help me bartend? It's good practice before you start next week as a bartender."

CJ pauses, surprised but grinning. "Does that mean you're telling me I'm getting promoted?"

I chuckle and nod my head. "You've been doing great. We're just formalizing it a bit. We want to start your official training next week."

His face lights up. "Thanks! I appreciate it, and I'd love to help out with the party."

He nods toward the backroom. "Anyway, I should get this to Chef. Catch you later." And with that, he's off, walking faster to deliver the box.

I watch him go, then turn back to Callie, feeling a bit more optimistic. Despite the chaos and backlog, I trust my team—especially her.

"Anything else you need help with? If not, Drew's here, and I'm guessing it's to finish the meal plan."

I glance over at the security camera and see Drew entering the bar area.

"Nope, that'll be all! I'll finalize the menu with Drew and let Chef know. Thanks, Callie!"

I'd texted Drew about an hour ago, asking him to come in when he had a chance so that we could discuss the BBQ and catch up. He's been in town for just over a year now. Despite some rocky times early on, he's become a close friend. Now he's got an unplanned baby almost here, and I get how terrifying that can be—even if our situations aren't remotely the same.

"Hey, man," I greet him as I step out. "Beer?"

He shakes his head. "Nah, but I'd love a tavern burger."

"On it!" Callie calls from behind me.

"So," I start, busying myself by pouring him a glass of ice water. "Callie offered to bartend and handle the food setup—with CJ's help. I was thinking we could include all of Liv's favorites, plus some extras. I know you said she didn't really want a baby shower or birthday party, so instead of calling it that and risking her getting worked up, we're considering calling it just a 'summer kickoff' party."

I pause briefly before adding, "But the idea is still to celebrate her, too."

"Sounds good," he says with a laugh. "I think she'd be fine with that—or at least happy once she's there and realizes what it is. And tell Maisie thank you, too."

He pauses, then looks at me sincerely. "Can't believe you're planning a party right after everything that happened... It's a lot more than most would, but I really appreciate it, man."

"Yeah... It's been a really fucking crazy week, but I think it'll be okay. We need to have family around, you know? Jake could use some normalcy, too—and fun. He's mostly been surrounded by one of the guys all the time, and while he loves them, I think he's starting to realize things aren't exactly normal."

"No kidding. Lincoln's been burning the midnight oil trying to figure out how Stephanie pulled all this off. I know Hayes talked to you—but I can't say I don't disagree with Lincoln. Something's not adding up. She's not exactly the sharpest tool in the shed..."

"So you think the person she's working with is?" I ask, trying to piece together his meaning.

"Someone came up with a nearly foolproof plan to get Jake —and they're ballsy. Taking risks in broad daylight, playing up that 'right under your nose' thing. Big picture? I don't know what the end game is, but Stephanie asking for a few million wired to some bogus offshore account? There's definitely something we're missing."

"But what? I don't have any issues with anyone—no unpaid debts, no hidden gambling addictions. Honestly, I don't know who would come after us like that... or why they would."

He pauses, tone firm. "We'll figure it out."

I nod, swallowing hard, trying to shake off the heaviness lingering in the conversation. I've been obsessing over the who's, why's, and what's for days now, and my mind keeps coming up blank.

Rather than dwell any longer on the unknowns, I shift to a safer topic. "So, you getting excited about the baby?"

"Sure," he says, then cringes. "To be straight up? I'm terrified... Ellie and Ben I've got down, but a baby? The first baby I ever held was August."

I can't help but chuckle, "Yeah, I felt the same way with Jake."

"Got any advice for me?" Drew asks, voice quiet but curious.

I hesitate, trying to find the right words. There are a million things I could say, but I settle on something broad and impactful. "Honestly, I was pretty much thrown into this without the eight months to prepare. I never got a chance to steady myself. But... I'll never forget what Coach told me the day I said I wasn't resigning. I thought he'd be pissed—here I was, in my prime; they'd offered tens of millions, and I just said... no. When I explained why, he just nodded... and went really quiet...

I take a breath, trying to recall every detail exactly. "He looked at me and said, 'I know you. I know you're doing what you think is right. That's honorable, but I want you to really listen—and really understand this. One day...'" I pause, swallowing hard. "'One day, that kid's gonna sit across from someone and tell them what it was like to be raised by you. Make sure it's a story worth telling. Worth remembering. Worth being proud of. Otherwise, you've just thrown away a lifetime career and millions of dollars for a kid who would've been fucked up either way.'"

Drew's head pulls back a little, eyes wide. "Damn," he mutters. "That's..."

"Yeah, maybe a little harsh," I admit. "But it really stuck with me. Made me think. You know, someday Jake's gonna be out there, telling his future wife about his childhood. And it could be mostly defined by Stephanie—her bullshit, her lack of parenting. Or it could be filled with all the good memories I've made with him. I guess, I don't know... I just feel pretty damn blessed, knowing he's living a life most kids never will. Yeah, I have my bad days, my parenting doubts. But overall? We're lucky. We've got each other. We get to live here. He's got my family—Ellie, Ben—and everyone else we call family, too. Hell, the whole town feels like one big family. Like he's got a village. And now, after everything with Maisie... it's like it's all falling into place, how it's supposed to be."

Drew lets that hang for a moment, then chuckles softly. "Oof. Isn't that the dream? Giving your kids a better life than you had. I want that for my kids, too. But it sucks knowing Ellie and Ben will still have that trauma—losing a parent so young."

He pauses, deep in thought. "Charlie and I lost our parents when... fuck, they weren't even much older than I am now— barely in their forties. Seemed ancient back then, but now I realize I'll probably be around that age when Ben hits his teens... I can't even wrap my head around what that must've been like for them—losing everything so early."

I nod along, feeling choked up all of a sudden.

"I've always felt for kids losing their dads. And Olivia losing her partner. But now I wonder—I don't think I ever really grieved for Dan, losing his wife and kids."

He shakes his head softly, then shrugs. "Anyway, fuck—I

digress. You're right, though. That coach had a piece of advice I could think about in a hundred different ways."

"Yeah," I say after a moment, still thinking about when we lost Dan and the impact it had on all of us. "You know, when Dan died, it really brought that advice back to the front of my mind, too. It's a different kind of sad when you're a parent, and you realize how fragile life really is. I know Jake would be okay without me; I know my family would step in and help, but..."

"But it's not the life he's supposed to have," Drew finishes quietly for me.

I nod, feeling that weight settle again. Sometimes the truth hits hard, but deep down, it's what keeps us honest—what we need to remember.

Chapter Twenty-Seven

Maisie

"Ahhhh!" Jake's shouts echo from the backyard, making me look up from the brownie batter I'm mixing. He's in the backyard, grinning and soaked from head to toe. Ethan and Jake have been out there for the last hour, 'preparing for the most epic battle ever,' as Jake keeps saying. They've got a few dozen—fast-fill—water balloon packs, all kinds of water guns, thirty-gallon drums of water strategically scattered around the yard, hoses, and I'm pretty sure I don't even want to know what else.

Ethan planned the whole party and kept saying I didn't need to do anything. He hired a house cleaner yesterday, Chef Julian whipped up all the food, and Callie is doing all the set up right now with CJ's help. They've been going in and out, upstairs and downstairs making sure the bar out back is fully stocked, and the tables are ready for when we want to eat.

Meanwhile, I'm over here nervously baking. This is the first real 'outing' Ethan and I are doing—basically announcing to everyone that we're a thing. *Again? For the first time? I'm not really sure.* But either way, the rumors have been flying around all week, and while we haven't exactly shot them down, this feels like a real step. The right step, actually.

I haven't asked Ethan if I can move in yet. My plan is to bring it up today, after the party—just casually, maybe. But the more I think about it, the more the nerves start creeping in. Doubts I know I shouldn't be feeling but still can't seem to kick.

I go back to the brownies, pouring the batter into the pans and sticking them in the oven. When I glance up again, two more faces are bolting into the yard.

Brody and Jody sprinting toward Ethan and Jake. Melody's trailing behind, the youngest, looking equally as excited, but not nearly as fast as her older siblings.

As I walk down the stairs to see them, Margie's already hugging Ethan, her frame nearly swallowed by his. She laughs at something he says, but I don't quite hear it. Although I do hear her say, "Finally, only took you a decade!" For a brief second, a little bit of sadness tickles my throat. They've always gotten along so well, and I'd thought I'd have that with Jason, but... it never quite happened.

I glance over at him, my feet hitting the last step, and he's standing nearest to me. He's got the whole Jason Statham look about him, and considering his name, he just loves to hear when people say he looks like him.

"Well, well, if it isn't Miss Virtue playing house with her ex-boyfriend," Jason teases with a grin. I try to laugh, even if I don't think the joke's that funny.

Ethan straightens up behind him, his face flickering with annoyance—as if sensing the tension between us.

Margie rolls her eyes and flicks Jason's arm, used to the antics. "Cut it out," she admonishes. "Let Maisie be happy."

Melody's the first of the kids to spot me. She squeals and rushes over, throwing her arms around me in a big hug. The others wave from a distance, already plotting their attack for the water fight. Jody and Brody are bouncing on their toes, trying not to look too eager, while Jody whispers something to Brody under her breath, eyes glinting with mischief.

"Thanks for coming!" I call after Melody as she scampers off again, already heading straight for the chaos.

I scan the yard, noticing one of Margie's brood isn't here—Cody. I raise an eyebrow.

"Where's Cody?" I ask, casually, even though I already know the answer.

"Friend's house," Margie shrugs with a small smile. "He's apparently too cool for us."

I grin, nudging her. "Maybe for you, but never for his favorite aunt..."

Brody pipes up from off to the side, yelling, "Only aunt!"

"Semantics!" I shout back, laughing.

Olivia, Drew, and the kids roll right in after that. Olivia doesn't even slow down—she heads straight for the cupcakes; her eyes already narrowing on the prize, like it's her mission.

"They're beautiful! All these pinks and purples," she says with a big grin, snagging a plate and already digging in.

Drew watches her with a soft smile. "Peonies, and I didn't even need to apologize," he teases, wiggling his eyebrows at her.

"Oh my god, they are! You did this?" Olivia asks, eyes shining with genuine admiration toward him.

He laughs, shaking his head. "I only hired Maisie. The flavor and frosting—that's all her."

"Well, I took some artistic liberty with you in mind. They're chocolate—" I start to say.

"Chai!" she interrupts excitedly, mumbling with her mouth full as she takes a bite, clearly loving them.

"Yes!"

"I'm obsessed! I want these every year for the rest of my life," she declares, eyes wide.

Drew raises his hand for a high five, and I smack it hard.

"Nailed it, Maisie. Hiring you anytime I need help fightin' crazy ladies or feedin' pregnant ones," he says with a wink.

Olivia's mouth drops open, a piece of cupcake almost falling out. "Andrew!"

I can't help but laugh and do a little bow. What can I say? I even surprised myself with actually using the skills Luke taught me.

Twenty minutes later and the backyard is alive with almost everyone we love. I know that they all have parties like this regularly, but after Ethan got back, I always opted out, and for the first time I'm regretting it. I missed out on *years* of this, because of my stubbornness and the thought puts a damper on my mood.

I end up back inside, heavy feet carrying me back to the immaculately clean kitchen. If I could get away with baking something, I would. But I have a feeling that Ethan would catch me before I even preheated the oven and ask what's wrong.

Searching for something to do, anything, I settle on making myself an iced coffee—because what goes better with anxiety than caffeine, right? I opt for honey and vanilla, and take it to the front porch where I could sit in a rocker and greet everyone that comes.

As soon as I sit, I hear the rumblings of a truck and look to see it's Hayes and Charlie. Relief floods through me, and I set my coffee down to go swoop in and steal August. He's at that adorable stage—big smiles, no stranger danger yet, just pure innocence.

"Look at you livin' up on the hill, looking down at us peasants." Hayes says with a knowing grin as he places the carseat carrier over his forearm.

Charlie must see the blush hitting my cheeks, because she says, "Ignore him."

"Will do! Please tell me August isn't sleeping so I can get some baby snuggles?"

"He's all yours," Hayes says handing me the carseat. "Guys out back?" Before I can answer he's hustling toward the side of the house, and I can't help but laugh.

We settle onto the front porch and a few minutes later Odessa pops her head around the corner. "Found y'all! Who're ya hiding from up here?"

"Everyone?" Charlie laughs and I nod.

"Good enough for me," Odessa takes the seat next to me. "How are you holding up, Maisie?"

"I'm—" I start to say good, but I'm clearly not feeling the best right now "Overwhelmed?"

They both nod, as if they understand.

Odessa sighs heavily. "No one talks about how, despite getting everything you could ever want, it doesn't mean the insecurities from before just disappear."

"Yeah... and I feel guilty for being stubborn. Regretful of wasting all that time because I was so stuck in my own head..." I admit softly.

Charlie chuckles and points at me. "You may have us beat on timelines... but you're talking to someone who moved across the country and didn't tell anyone," she says, pointing at herself. "And someone who went on, what, a four-month silent treatment—cold shoulder—because of pure stubbornness. You're in good company, girl. We get it."

"Stubborn women make the world go around. Can't convince me otherwise," Odessa adds, pausing thoughtfully. "You don't have to regret those feelings just because they might not be valid anymore. That doesn't mean they weren't once valid to you."

"Hindsight and all that," I reply, nodding.

"All those feelings are natural. Let 'em come and go. The intrusive thoughts? They can be a storm holding you down—or just a cloud floating by. Let it be the cloud," Odessa says gently.

"That's actually pretty good advice," I admit.

"Lots and lots of therapy," Charlie teases with a grin.

Odessa nods in agreement. "Years upon years, girl."

Charlie glances at me with a knowing look. "So... you gonna talk to Ethan about moving in?"

I hesitate, a little unsure. "Yeah, I think so. I mean, I want to. Is it crazy to say I'd marry him tomorrow if he wanted to?"

Charlie smiles softly. "Nope. You're a natural mom already. Just saying."

I laugh. "Not sure we're *there* yet. But..." I trail off, feeling a little unsure but hopeful.

Odessa nudges me playfully. "Well, if Ethan has his way, it won't be long before you're pregnant," she teases, and I feel a little flushed. But truthfully? With Ethan? It doesn't scare me. Not one bit.

The sound of tires on the pavement draws our attention to see the "bod squad" pulling up—carpooling in Cooper's Durango. Liam, Leo, Delta, and Lincoln pile out, laughing and joking. I lean forward on the porch to get a better look. It's hilarious—"That isn't even a small car, and yet they look like absolute giants climbing out of it," I mutter with a smirk before handing August back to his mom.

Odessa laughs, "Can't deny it is a good-looking group of men."

I walk out to greet them, only to see Cooper open the trunk and reveal another arsenal full of water guns.

"Cooper! What the heck did you bring?"

"*Maisie*, we had so much fun at the store," he insists, his smile spreading mischievously, like a kid who just found out they get to stay up all night for the first time.

Delta groans next to him. "They bought it all."

Then Leo comes around the other side of the car. "Delta, pull the stick out of your—" he pauses, then looks at me and cringes. "Sorry, Maisie. Forgot you don't cuss."

"No judgment from me," I say with a smile. "But I have to agree. It's a party, Delta. Don't be a pooper."

I help them carry the new supply of weapons out to the backyard, even though I'm only carrying a stray gun that fell out of one of the tubs.

Ethan greets me with a quick kiss. "Ready to feed these people?"

I nod, and he yells, "FOOD'S READY! Everyone upstairs so we can eat—and then get the party started!"

Everett is standing in line in front of me, with Odessa right ahead of him. She's trying to scoop a smoked bacon meatball with a serving spoon, but it keeps falling off.

"T-T-T-TODAY JUNIOR!"

She spins around, wielding the serving spoon like a weapon. "Everett, I will cut you... in the name of Jesus."

"Adam Sandler against Anjelah Johnson? Come on, Dess! Not even a comedian comparison."

"Luke!" Odessa yells, "Can you fire him?"

Luke, rightfully so, grins and jokingly says "Sorry, Astor. You're fired."

Everett mockingly gasps, "How the turn tables..."

Olivia bumps into me and I turn to her, and see she's got that same grin that Cooper had earlier. "Watch this," she mouths.

She spins around "OHMYGOD! Oh. My god." She grabs her belly, looking down panicked. Every man, except for Levi stands up immediately and has shocked faces. Cooper behind us drops his plate on to the food table. Drew nearly trips over the ottoman trying to get to her. And then she grins, "Just kidding."

"Boots..." Drew groans, looking both relieved and terrified.

The house has people all over it, eating and drinking. Shouts and jokes are made. Kids eat as quickly as they can, so they can go back outside to play.

By the time everyone has eaten, the crowd has dwindled to just the core group of us—minus Odessa and Luke, who excused themselves, insisting Luke had work to do. But we all see through that lie.

I'm just finishing my last bite of watermelon salad when Callie comes over. "I'll finish cleaning this up and head out, if that's cool with you guys? I think CJ can handle the drinks and the bar outside."

"Are you sure you don't want to stay?" I ask, hoping she'll choose to hang out a bit longer. I've always genuinely liked Callie, but I had to keep my distance because of how close she is to Ethan. It's nice that I can finally be her friend again.

Callie takes a long look at all the guys and smirks. "Nope. Those guys are dangerous, and my self-control around hot men is teeny-tiny. Plus, I'm exhausted—I just want to go home and curl up on the couch with some trash TV."

Can't say I blame you, girl.

Ethan rolls his eyes, mumbling something along the lines of, "You and the bod squad..." Then he sighs. "You're good to go whenever. Thanks for all your help today, Cal."

He stands up from the enormous dining room table and announces loudly, "It is time!" As if on cue, everyone scurries around, rushing down the stairs and out into the backyard.

It doesn't take long before chaos erupts—a whirlwind of splashing water, laughter, and squeals. Over twenty people dash and dart, firing water guns in every direction, while water balloons fly through the air like mini projectiles. The sounds of splashes and shrieks mix with playful shouts, filling the air with energy.

Amidst the frenzy, the "moms" of the group—Olivia, Charlie, Margie, Isla, and Liam—sit back comfortably on the porch, watching the pandemonium with amused smiles, sipping drinks as the chaos unfolds.

In the thick of it, Cooper is in an all-out brawl with the other guys, cartoonishly ducking, dodging, and firing. His teammate? Ellie who is sitting confidently on his back and shooting at everyone with gleeful energy. Cooper doesn't break character as he carries her, weaving through the mayhem, pretending he's a fearless hero on a daring rescue, narrowly escaping the villains in the wild. That is, until a water balloon smacks him square in the chest. Without missing a beat, he goes full action-movie style—dramatic fall, arms flailing, carefully landing to avoid hurting Ellie, who's giggling uncontrollably the entire time.

I team up with Jake—we go for sneaky, quiet tactics, quietly sneaking around and launching surprise attacks. We hit Delta square in the chest with a well-aimed water balloon, catching him completely off guard, causing him to drop the balloons he was carrying.

"Rookie mistake, Delta!" I hear Charlie shout from the safety of her seat.

"Motherfu..." he groans and looks up to see who threw it. I duck behind the water barrel and pull Jake down, so he can't see us.

I glance the other way to see Lincoln has paired up with Brody and Melody, strategizing behind the bushes on the far side of the house. I had noticed Jody, was acting like a free agent, running wild, splashing and throwing water balloons everywhere, laughing wildly—the typical middle child.

Meanwhile, Everett is running full throttle, yelling loudly, "Get to the choppa!" and "Say hello to my little friend!" as he vaults over obstacles, totally immersed in the madness.

Drew and Ben are nowhere to be seen—yet somehow, they manage to sneak around, launching water balloons and sniping with the electric water guns, hitting their targets with near-perfect timing.

I spin around as best I can while crouching, searching for Ethan. He's been all over the place, but now he's gone completely silent—too quiet. Then I see him. He's sitting with his back against one of the water drums, holding some type of super-soaker, a grin stretched wide across his face. He's just waiting there, oblivious to the chaos around him, like he's a guy who just found out he won the lottery. The pure joy, love, and devotion radiating from him is undeniable, and I swear I can feel it from over here.

He winks, and before I can even blink, he jumps up and totally drenches Jason—who's mostly stayed out of the fray but somehow thought he could sneak up on Ethan. The loud cackle that escapes me feels spontaneous, uncontrollable, as I watch Jason walk away, pouting and dripping. Ethan's the only guy here who's not military-trained, but he's also a former pro athlete—tough, agile, and so freakin'... sexy.

Then, out of nowhere, Hayes douses us with a super-soaker as he runs by laughing. And just like that, we're back in the game.

Chapter Twenty-Eight

Maisie

Finally, things start to slow down a bit. The kids are just hanging out now—most of them sprawled in the grass, giggling, chasing each other, some on the play structure swinging and climbing. The chaos of the water fight has mostly faded, as everyone's opted to dry out in the sun.

CJ has been behind the bar all afternoon, but now he's finishing up and getting ready to go—something I'm sure Jason isn't too happy about. Jason's been sulking over there since Ethan bested him earlier, grumbling to CJ, who looks less than interested. Margie mentioned they know each other somehow, but I'm assuming it's mainly because Jason often hangs out at Ponderosa.

Most of the guys have disappeared upstairs, likely fawning over Ethan's fancy whiskey collection—though Ethan doesn't even drink it.

The atmosphere feels lighter, more relaxed. I lean against the back of my cushioned chair, watching the kids and listening to the low hum of conversations drifting around us.

And then Isla nearly screeches at Charlie. "Oh my god! You haven't read Willow Aster?"

"Which series are you talking about?" I ask, amused.

Isla snaps her fingers, trying to think. "The single dad... Something players?"

"Oh! I read those," I say. "I guarantee Ethan has them upstairs."

Isla's eyes go wide. "Wait, Ethan reads them?"

Charlie nods mockingly, smirking. "Of course he does. If Maisie even breathed near something, Ethan was all over it."

"Pretty much," I chuckle. "Apparently, he also went through a phase of buying anything he overheard me talking about."

Charlie laughs, leaning back and raising her hands. "Not that I play around with the word 'stalker,'" she grins, "but..."

"Charlie!" Isla scoffs, playfully scolding her. "That's not the same at all!" Then she turns to me with excited eyes, "What else did he buy?"

I laugh and gesture toward the house behind me. "Besides the house? I have no idea how long the list is. I do know how he knows what books I like, though—he followed my Goodreads account. Anything I give a four- or five-star rating, he buys." That's almost everything, considering I only rate books I really love.

Charlie snorts. "That's... kind of oddly romantic." It really is, and kind of adorable—and probably cost a pretty penny. When I asked if he'd actually read any of them, he just shrugged, saying "not really." But I caught the faintest blush, and I couldn't help but wonder if maybe, just maybe, he knew what a total smutty smut reader I am.

"I'll be right back." I push off the chair and head inside, feeling so grateful for this crazy, wonderful life. Ethan's back—completely—and I've got the best friend group, plus more, who feel like family. It's everything my eighteen-year-old self could've dreamed of.

As I walk through the house, I hear a voice—familiar and warm as ever. "Hey, My Perfect Maisie! Where ya headed?"

I glance over my shoulder to see Ethan, sitting casually in the formal dining room, his face lit up with that trademark easy smile—even with all his friends nearby, he looks just happy.

"Library," I say softly, smiling. "Gotta grab a book for Charlie."

Hayes raises his eyebrows and grins knowingly. "Hell yeah! Make it a good one, Maisie."

I laugh and call over my shoulder as I start to walk again, "Oh, don't worry! It's even a series."

Cooper's the one to respond, yelling from his spot near the window, his voice booming down the hall. "Bring one for me too!"

I can't help but laugh harder, feeling the full blessing of this chapter in my life. I was feeling down earlier—overwhelmed by that storm cloud of regret—and I let it pass, just like Odessa suggested. Right now, all I see are blue skies and sunshine.

Stepping into the library, my good mood only multiplies. Right here, this space is a reminder: Ethan never gave up hope, even when I did. The house, the life, the dreams—they're all built on that quiet, unwavering patience he has. If that isn't the most endearing—crazy-in-the-best-way—thing in the world, I don't know what is.

The room is flooded with light—big windows on the side that let in the sun—and despite the thousands of books lining the shelves, the space doesn't feel dull or stuffy. Instead, it's lively, full of personality. Every shelf has its knickknacks, tiny framed photos, even a few quirky little trinkets I've never seen anywhere else. It feels more like a cozy, curated treasure trove than a library—and, it's truly better than any bookstore I've ever been in. And I didn't even have to marry the beast to get it (though, okay, the size and long hair might be a clue).

He has the entire room floor-to-ceiling, bookshelves in perfect alphabetical order. No chaos here—just neat rows of paperbacks and hardcovers, waiting to be pulled and explored.

I scan along each row, my fingers running lightly over the spines, searching for the series I have in mind. It's funny—libraries can often feel dark and cramped, but this one—this room—is full of light and life. I find myself smiling, even as I move in a quiet concentration.

Finally, I touch the spine of the book I was after—an ironic choice considering my current housing situation, shacking up with a former football player that's a single dad.

"Just the person I was hoping I'd stumble upon here."

Without turning around, I recognize CJ's voice and the subtle click of the door closing quietly behind him, and even quieter—the soft sound of a lock clicking into place.

Oh, no. Nooo. No.

My senses instantly sharpen, the air in the room suddenly thick with tension. Memories flood in—unwanted, invasive. It's as if my body remembers this space, the feelings I'd rather forget, and is acting on its own accord. My heart pounds just a little faster, and I feel that familiar rush of nerves that always build when I'm about to have a panic attack.

"Hey!" I call out, trying to keep my voice steady, throwing a glance over my shoulder. "One sec—I'm just looking for a book for Charlie."

It might be paranoia. It might be that strange, primal gift of fear. Whatever it is, my eyes fixate on the purple geode, blood pounding in my ears. Without a second thought, I inch it back, fingertips trembling as I press the button beneath. I watch, heart racing, as I casually slide it forward again—as if I were simply adjusting its placement.

Please, dear God work.

Unless, maybe I'm overreacting?

Doesn't matter.

Trust.

Your.

Gut.

"Maisie." He says, and I can tell he's right behind me; feel the hot air from his breath tickling the hairs on my neck, and I want to scream.

I turn, trying to keep my body as close to the shelves as I can as to not touch him. The smug look on his face is enough to send chills down my spine.

"I need a favor."

Still trying to play it cool, I attempt to smile and respond, but my voice only comes out strangled.

Clearing my throat, I try again. "What's up?"

"You're going to stay very quiet and help me, or else not only will you die, so will Jake. I actually have a friend with him right now." Then he lifts his shirt, and I see the gun in his belt holster. He doesn't unclip it, only uses it as a taunting measure. *Could I knock him out before he can get it? Maybe? But he's got height and weight on me.*

"A friend?" I breathe.

He winks and then smiles. *I was just down there, playing outside, we know everyone down there. Trust them all. Right?* Then it hits me, Jason. He was talking to Jason the entire time.

"What do you want, CJ?"

"I'm not wasting time explaining anything. Just fucking open it, so I can leave!"

"Open what?!"

"The safe!" *The... what?*

"Safe?" I ask desperately.

He gestures behind me toward the large scenic watercolor painting on the wall, the one I loved so much.

"The one behind the pines."

Dumbly, I answer. "I don't have the combination."

"You're smart." He says and grabs me by the arm yanking me toward the other side of the room. "I'm sure you'll figure it out."

He half drags me toward the photo, and my jaw drops when he pulls on the right side, the painting opening toward us so wide I stumble back, and sure enough there's a large safe set into the wall.

"Is this for real?" *What crazy movie did I just step into?* I'm being used as a hostage and there's a giant safe with a number key pad, and a spinny wheel.

He ignores me completely, but I turn to look at him. Nothing about his face says this is a joke, and I can't help but feel a chill down my spine.

"Open it."

My hand gingerly reaches out, and it feels like betrayal of all betrayals. One, I have no idea what Ethan even keeps in here. Two, I can't really give it over to this insane person, right? But he threatened Jake. And maybe, maybe Jason is in on it? Unless CJ was lying about having an accomplice. The problem is, I don't know, and I don't know if I can take the chance.

Code, think of the code. I type in Jake's birthday, but it only beeps angrily, and the red blinks back at me. Then I try my birthday and again nothing.

Tears immediately fill my eyes as I glance at him.

"Try again," he demands, and my body immediately trembles as I see him pull his gun out of the holster.

I scramble, trying as many variations as I can think of, my fingers moving quickly and deftly, but nothing works.

"Figure it out!" he growls angrily in my ear. In my peripheral vision, I see him raising his pistol toward my head.

Chapter Twenty-Nine

Ethan

This is one of those surreal, life is damn good, moments. There's a party in the backyard of the fancy house, that I built for my girl—the same girl I finally got back. The 90's country music is being drowned out by kids laughing and playing. I'm sitting at the huge dining table with the guys, and I gotta say, I'm thankful I splurged on the extra-large one. I had hopes it would be used for moments like this, where I just get to enjoy the good vibe, but I hadn't known how perfect it'd be.

Cooper leaned back in his chair, a wry grin tugging at his mustache. "You know," he said with a chuckle, "I never thought I'd see the day when I'd have such a 'domesticated' life. Used to be out there in the wild, doing cool shit—night dives, armor, guns—completely different world."

Hayes raised an eyebrow, a smirk playing on his face. "Yeah, well, I've heard the rumors from Ponderosa Pine. And let me tell you—'domesticated' isn't exactly the word I'd use. Unless, of course, it involves a different woman every weekend...."

I folded my arms, nodding. "Yeah, I've heard the same

rumors," I said with a small grin. "Sounds more like he's traded the 'wild shit' for... well, an S.T.D.."

Cooper laughed, shaking his head. "Oh fuck off. I'm careful. It's Liam ya gotta worry about. He's been sneaking off at all times of the night and won't tell us where he's going."

Hayes and I both looked at Liam, who's been his normal, quiet self. He only shrugs, and plays it off with a smirk.

"Liam, you dog!" Hayes chuckles, "You gettin' some and not telling us?"

Then all three phones—Cooper's, Hayes's, and Liam's—go off at once. Not just a ping, but a full-blown chime, like they're all synchronized. And everyone, except me, shifts immediately. The smiles on their faces faded so quickly that you wouldn't have known, two seconds ago, we were all laughing. I start patting my pockets, looking for my phone, but then I remember it's plugged in and running the music out back.

"East wing. Alarm was set off less than one minute ago, two subjects in a seemingly intense conversation." That's the line I catch as my gaze involuntarily goes out the window to where my phone is surely going off as well. The yard's still busy, kids running around, laughing, totally oblivious. But Drew, he gets that look—like he's just stiffened up, back straight as an arrow. He's looking at his phone, so I guess he got the same alert. Whatever he says makes everyone stop mid-play, all eyes on him.

There's this thick tension rolling off him that I can't place. I glance at Lincoln next—he's glued to his phone, looking serious, too—and then I notice Everett. The smile that's usually easy on his face falters. *Something's wrong. Bad wrong.*

Amid all this, I vaguely catch Hayes barking out orders to Cooper, Liam, and Delta. But honestly? It's like they're speaking another language. Their words are sharp, clipped, tactical. When I turn back to the room, I see all three already have guns in hand, ready now, and the realization hits me hard —something serious is happening. *Here. Right, now. In my house. And I don't have Maisie or Jake with me.*

"What the hell is going on?!" I demand, slamming my hands down on the table. It's loud, probably too loud, but I don't care. I need answers.

Hayes locks eyes with me—loaded, steady, not messing around. "You trust me?"

I splutter almost instantly, my stomach twisting. My eyes dart toward the yard again. Nothing. No one. Just an empty yard and shadows.

"Ethan," Hayes snaps. "Do you trust me?" *Fuck.*

I swallow hard, feeling my throat tighten. "Yeah, fuck! I trust you."

"Then you're gonna sit right there while we handle this as a team."

"What? No—what are you talking about? I need to help."

"Maisie hit the panic button in your library."

What? My heart slams against my ribcage, like I've been punched. I feel breathless, weightless—sucked dry of air. My head whips around, fingers trembling as I start to stand.

"Sit your ass down and don't make this even harder on us," Hayes cuts in, his voice cold as steel.

A hand suddenly slams onto my shoulder, holding me in place. I look up—and all I see is sadness in Liam's eyes, like he's begging me to listen to Hayes.

"You're wasting time. Her time. And I swear if I have to argue with you about it... I will have Liam knock your ass out."

"Just go!" I grind out, my fists naturally ball, about to explode, but I stay seated. The frustration feels like it's boiling over—threatening to blind me with rage. I feel like I've been benched, helpless. I hate it, but what else am I supposed to do? This is real life, and I have no idea what the hell is going on with Maisie and who is in the library with her.

Two quick motions with Hayes's fingers, and Liam, Cooper, and Delta follow him out. All trained, smooth, ready. I can't help but respect that. Me? I want to grab my gun, run after them, throw myself into the chaos.

Instead, I sit at this beautiful table I picked out and fucking hope that SEAL Team Cascadia County is enough to keep Maisie and Jake safe.

Chapter Thirty

Maisie

My whole body feels frozen, like I can't really move or breathe right. A strange numbness is creeping in, making everything slow and heavy—like the start of a panic attack. *No, I can do this!*

"It's okay, you're okay, breathe," I hear Levi softly talking me through it as I focus on inhaling and exhaling. It couldn't have lasted more than a few seconds, but I see the gun trembling in CJ's hand, as if he's losing his patience.

I quickly type in more numbers, letting the chaos of memories spin wildly—birthdays, anniversaries, the day he was drafted to the NFL—all flashing through my mind in a jumbled mess.

I've already gone through all of those—what am I forgetting?

My chest tightens again, like some invisible vice is squeezing the air from my lungs. Our anniversary? Do we even have one? I start punching in every important date I can think of, even trying graduation day twice. Then it hits me—the day before. The night we confessed it all.

My index finger shakes as I hover over 0611, hesitating. Just as I'm about to press the last number, a loud bang rings out —so deafening that I suck in a startled gasp. At the same moment, something warm and wet splatters across the side of my face. The metallic taste of blood fills my mouth and I realize it must be open and gaping, but I can't focus on that. All I see is the large body suddenly crumpling to the ground.

My body feels locked tight now, the tremors gone. I stare at the red splattered across my outstretched arm, then out of the corner of my eye, I notice the blood covering the wall behind where CJ once stood—brain matter and blood mixing as smells I can't quite make sense of hit my nose.

Who? How?

I don't dare move, not even an inch, trying to stay perfectly still. That is, until I hear the steadiness but complete sorrow in Coopers voice as he says, "Clear." *Oh, Cooper.*

My knees instantly go weak, threatening to buckle, but I manage to turn around, being cognizant of the fact there's a dead body at my feet that I don't want to look at or trip over.

I scan the library starting with the main door, but I can't make sense of where that shot came from. That is, until I get to the corner of the room on the far wall, where the bottom half of the bookshelves are askew.

The secret door to Jake's room is slightly wedged open, and Cooper is kneeling with his pistol held steady on CJ's lifeless form. I stare at the sorrow etched on his face, and a new wave of guilt begins to eat at me, sobs threatening to break free from my gut, rising into my chest.

The top half of the door is pried open the rest of the way, and Cooper lowers his shoulders and head to go underneath, remaining in the same position, with his eyes fixed on the target.

Hayes steps behind him, his left hand moving to his shoulder, and, in a calm, resigned voice, he utters the same word Cooper just did. "Clear."

Cooper looks up, nods once, and then lowers his gun before standing up.

Meanwhile, I stare at them like a deer caught in headlights, unable to make sense of what's going on as my chest heaves and tears prick my eyes.

"You're okay, Maisie." Hayes tries to comfort, his hand extended slightly in my direction, but neither of them move in my direction.

My body seemingly unlocks with his words, and I run to Cooper, throwing myself at him and wrapping my arms around his shoulders.

"Cooper, whatever the heck your full name is, you just saved my life." Tears stream down my face, and I let them.

"Not even nearly dying can get you to cuss, huh?" He wraps his arms around me, and I swear I hear him laugh before adding, "And, it's Dane Cooper Bradley."

"Dane Cooper Bradley... your first name isn't even Cooper?!" I shout a little too loudly.

"Nah, middle. And with my initials being D.B.—Cooper was a pretty natural nickname."

"Dane..." I try it and quickly shake my head. "They're right, you're a Cooper."

"Come on" he lets go with one arm, but slides the other across my shoulder blades to guide me out. "Don't look back, let's get you out of here."

"Wait! He said... He said he was working with someone," Cooper and Hayes both still, "And.. And I think it's Jason."

Hayes is hitting buttons on his phone so quickly that I can't even explain my reasoning.

"I don't—I don't know that for sure."

Cooper continues to walk me into Jake's room. "Better safe than sorry."

"Drew, Lincoln, and Everett have everyone in the game room."

"How do you want to handle it, boss?"

Hayes looks deep in thought. "Get 'em out of there like we don't know. Separate them somehow. Send the kids..."

The vibration on his phone has him trailing off... "Never mind. Lincoln handled it."

"Handled it?! How?!"

Hayes shrugs casually, "Choked him out."

Chapter Thirty-One

Ethan

Thump. Thump. Thump—the only sound in the quiet house is my heel pounding into the floor, my knee bouncing beneath the surface of the dining room table. Hayes and the guys are somewhere inside, probably coming up with a plan and getting ready to kick down doors—or whatever the fuck Navy SEALs do.

Meanwhile, I'm still sitting here, trying to make sense of what's even happening. Maisie pushed the panic button in the library—*what does that even mean? Could it have been an accident? Or is something really wrong? Was someone actually working with Stephanie, and now they're inside my house?* My stomach twists just thinking about it.

The house feels different—despite the large windows, it feels like the walls are closing in on me. *Is this how Maisie feels during a panic attack? Is this how Luke felt in the hospital?* I get it now—feeling stuck here, glued to the chair, every nerve-ending tingling.

Drew brought the kids inside; I watched him herd everyone in and scan the backyard—securing everything. Surely, he would know exactly where to go and how to keep them the safest. I trust him, trust Everett, and trust Lincoln with Jake's life. Honestly, I don't doubt for a second that Olivia, Charlie, and Isla would go to hell and back for everyone in that room, too. Still, I couldn't help but imagine the worst— a tiny gap, a sneaky crack someone could slip through. *What if there's a way in they don't know about? Or someone was already waiting inside, hidden in the shadows?*

My body itches to get up, run downstairs, grab my phone, and check the security feed—see what's going on. I know I shouldn't, I know I can't—at least, not without risking Hayes's plan. I should be afraid; I'm basically a sitting duck, out in the open, waiting. But deep down, my gut's telling me this isn't about me. There's a bigger plan, a calculated scheme—something not aimed directly at me, but around me. *But, what?*

My mind races, trying to understand why Maisie would push the panic button in the first place—if there's anything in that library anyone would want. There are random football collectibles, some stuff from my days playing or things I bought online, but nothing of real value. My desk is covered in paperwork—nothing of interest. The safe in the wall is mostly empty: a few grand, a Bowman Mickey Mantle card with an autographed ball that I bought from a friend, the house deed, some investment papers. Nothing that screams, 'Break into me for a massive payout.'

Unless the person was only after Maisie—though even then, it doesn't really make sense. Why target her when there are so many trained people around? It's all just chaos inside my head as my thoughts spiral and my heart pounds faster.

Still, even as I scream inwardly, outwardly I stay calm—a man sitting tense at the table, staring down the hallway, waiting.

For the first time, I regret the big house. I can't hear a damn thing, besides the muffled music out back—a slower country song, but I can't place the tune or care to.

Then I heard it— the distant sound of a gunshot. Nothing else. No yelling, no more shots, just silence. I wait, listening for more, for any noise apart from the stupid music outside, but it's only quiet.

My chest shudders, and I involuntarily gasp for air, not even realizing I'd been holding my breath—like that might somehow help me hear better.

It feels like forever before I hear footsteps down the hall. Then Delta appears in view, his face serious, but calm. "Maisie's safe. Physically unharmed. We got to her in time."

"What?" My voice sounds hoarse, uncertain.

"CJ." He ticks off the name with disgust. "He wanted her to open the safe you have."

My heartbeat ramps up, pounding loudly in my ears. "But, why?"

"I don't know. As soon as Cooper was in position and had a clear shot, he took it. I came to tell you as soon as Hayes gave the all-clear." Delta glances at his phone, but his expression remains unreadable, like he's not ready to share what he's seeing.

Then he lifts his gaze, and I can tell there's more. "What?"

"Jason's been implicated somehow, too." *Jason?*

Then it hits me hard, "He's with J—"

He interrupts me, calmly adding, "Jake's safe. Lincoln handled it." As if that explains any of what is going on.

"What does that mean?" I press, probably a little too aggressively. My hand hits the table, louder than expected, but Delta doesn't even blink.

He shrugs. "I don't know. But Lincoln's probably pissed he missed the CJ situation, add in Jason being involved..." he trails off, but I see the worry in his eyes.

Shuffling from the hallway has my gaze snapping up to see Maisie with Cooper's arm around her shoulder. I'm on my feet instantly, rushing toward her. She's as white as a ghost, but her eyes are bright—and, filled with love?

"Can I move in?" She blurts as she practically falls into me.

"What?" A nervous laugh comes out of me as my hands grip her hair and pull her into me. There are specks of blood covering her, but thankfully none look like they're from her.

"Can I move in?" She repeats. "After we redo that part of the library—and Luke does whatever investigation he needs to do."

"You don't really have a choice," I say, "You're stuck with us now."

"You should go check on Jake," she urges, her voice softer now. "Go see how he's doing."

"Come with me," I plead, desperation slipping into my tone.

Maisie hesitates, then shakes her head. "I'm covered in blood. I don't want him to see me like this. Luke's on his way; he'll want a statement, probably ask a billion questions."

I can't help the disappointment hitting me, even though I understand and agree that Jake shouldn't see her in this state.

"I've got her," Cooper assures me. "Check in with Hayes— see if it's okay for you to go down. Drew's got the basement totally locked down, and I don't want you opening that door and getting shot."

When I get to Jake's room, Hayes is on the phone, likely already talking to Luke. He looks up at me, voice steady but urgent. "Luke said the department's on their way. They should be here in about five minutes."

"Can I see Jake?" I ask, voice tight.

He nods. "They've got everyone safe in the theater room.

Everett's covering. Drew and Lincoln have Jason secured in the main section—away from them."

As I turn to leave, Hayes catches my arm. "Ethan... the kids don't know anything. Take a breath before you go storming in there and scaring them all."

"They don't know anything?" My voice comes out sharper than I intended.

He shrugs, like it's no big deal. "We're good at our job."

He goes back to talking to Luke, and I force myself to heed his warning. I take slow, deliberate steps down the hallway toward the stairs. Part of me is glad I didn't go into the library, didn't see CJ—yet another part whispers that I might regret holding back. *What did he want in the safe? Did I miss a chance to find out?*

When I get to the ground floor, I see Drew and Lincoln standing over Jason, who is hogtied on the floor. Jason's awake, just lying there, completely unharmed.

"They're okay," I tilt my head toward the movie room, hearing the muffled chaos of an animated film blasting through the door.

Drew nods back. "They're safe. They don't have a clue what's really happened—just that it's time to chill for a bit after all the craziness. Most of them are probably napping by now."

Hearing that, I take a deep breath and try to settle my nerves. Then I turn to Jason, the man I once called a friend. "What the hell is going on, Jason?"

"I don't know!" he blusters, voice strained. "These fucking guys are—"

Before he can finish, Drew drops in front of him so quickly, I barely see him move. His fist grips Jason's shirt, hauling him up effortlessly. "Keep your fucking voice down, or I'll knock your ass out longer than Lincoln did."

"About five minutes before the alarm went off," Lincoln

starts to explain, "Everett noticed him acting weird and started paying more attention, then the alarm sounded. We rushed everyone into the movie room. Everett was right—he was all jittery, checking his phone, moving around a lot—"

"You don't know shit," Jason cuts him off, glaring.

"Shut—the fuck—up," Drew demands, voice low but deadly.

"Look, we didn't know what was going on upstairs," Lincoln says, exasperated. "The fourth time he got up and started pacing, I discreetly pulled him out of the room."

Jason grunts and tries to shift again. "You strangled me, you bastard."

"You were acting like a tweaker," Drew replies coldly. "We. Don't. Take. Chances." I've seen Drew annoyed before—protective of Olivia after her accident, but never like this. Now, his jaw is clenched so tightly it looks like he's grinding his teeth, and his eyes are burning with fury. His entire body seems tense, like he's barely holding himself back from going full storm, ready to snap on Jason at any moment. *Can't say I blame him.*

Lincoln holds up a phone. "We checked his messages. Dozens to CJ—started the day Stephanie was arrested."

"What the fuck? Why?" I demand, my eyes locking on Jason—the guy I thought was a friend. Potentially even a brother-in-law someday.

"Don't know what you're talking about," Jason mutters from the ground.

Lincoln looks down at him. "He didn't delete a single message—shouldn't be hard to figure that out."

Jason remains silent on the floor, expression unreadable.

I swallow hard, looking to Lincoln. "What did CJ want in the safe?"

"The only text I saw related to that was this morning," Lincoln says, his voice low. He opens Jason's phone and continues scrolling. "Keep whatever fucking card and autograph. I only want the cash, and my name to stay out of it." *The Mickey Mantle card and ball?*

Lincoln looks up at me, eyes cold. "The next text describes every room in the house, and where the safe is in the library."

My heart sinks with betrayal. Jason knew all that because I stupidly hired him to paint the house when I moved back. I wanted to feel closer to Maisie—to have someone she loved and trusted help with the house I was building for her. But that asshole used it against me.

Loud footsteps boom down the stairs—definitely Luke. The man couldn't be quiet if his life depended on it.

"What the hell is going on?" Luke demands as soon as he hits the bottom step, his gaze flickering between us before settling on Jason. I see the same betrayal in his face that I know I'm wearing—it's a mirror of my own shock. "Jason, are you fucking kidding me? What did you do now?" Luke snaps, voice sharp and accusing.

I spin, facing Luke. "Now?!"

"Come on, Luke," Jason protests. "It's a setup. I didn't do shit!"

"Yeah, you said something similar a few weeks ago when the Crownovers said they were paying you to do some work at their place. You hadn't shown up yet, but you were cashing their checks like it was nothing. Told me it was all a misunderstanding." Luke's voice is steady, but I can hear the anger beneath it—more than just an accusation.

Lincoln perks up, eyes narrowing. "The Crownovers who have that cabin at Jackie's Lake?"

Luke's gaze sharpens, and suddenly, it clicks—the same light bulb we all just had. Jason had been working at the neighbors' house. Which means at some point, he must've seen CJ with Stephanie.

"Well, that explains how he figured it out before we did," Drew murmurs, voice low but knowing.

Lincoln's face twists in disgust—I've seen that look before. He's been struggling to figure out Stephanie's plans, to see who she was working with. The idea that Jason might've outplayed us could be what pushes him closer to the edge of that depressive spiral he's been fighting.

"Why?" I ask again, more forcefully this time, but Jason just stays silent, refusing to say a word.

Suddenly, I hear Deputy Ambrose calling down the stairs. "Sheriff?"

"Down here," Luke shouts back, shaking his head at Jason—looking like a disappointed dad who just found out his kid is actually a piece of shit.

Chapter Thirty-Two

Ethan

The next hour is a whirlwind of questions, loose plans, and shifting pieces. Everyone's trying to get a handle on what just happened and what comes next. The investigators are here now—searching the house, taking pictures, questioning everyone—trying to piece together exactly how this all went down. Luke had explicitly told me I was banned from the library and 'adjacent rooms', but he finally relented, agreeing to let me into Jake's room for a quick bag.

Jason was cuffed and taken away in the back of a squad car, without any real answers. He didn't even see his family, as they were tucked away in the movie room still. We didn't want the kids to see their dad arrested, but we did at least have Margie come out before. Luke explained it all, well the details we have pieced together, and she sobbed in his chest and then Maisie's.

Luke called Maisie's parents and they picked Maisie up to go to their house to shower and change. Then they came back and picked up Margie and the kids, so they could have a sleep-over at their house.

Meanwhile, I took the opportunity to pack up an overnight

bag for us all, grabbing some clothes, toiletries, and anything else I thought we might need. Then I gathered Jake, placed him in the Carrington's car, and headed back to Olivia and Drew's house with Hayes and Charlie. My parents had offered for us to stay with them tonight—somewhere safe, familiar, a place to breathe—and I'm just waiting on Maisie to decide what she wants to do.

For now, the Turner/Reynolds house feels like the best place to regroup. To sit and just breathe—at least until everything calms enough to make a real plan. One thing's clear: this isn't over, and we're only left with more questions.

Maisie arrives and immediately hugs Jake, then wraps her arms around me. She looks worn out, but I can tell the shower did her some good. Margie's with her too, eyes rimmed red but standing stoic. I hug her, saying I'm sorry—though I'm not even sure what I'm apologizing for, but it felt like the right thing to say.

The house hums like a beehive. Kids are blissfully unaware, all playing in Ben's room like everything's totally normal.

Lincoln has three laptops open in front of him, typing like a maniac. Margie found a spot at the corner of the table next to him, looking so small and helpless, sitting close and watching his screens in almost a daze.

Delta and Leo are bouncing conspiracy theories back and forth, trying to make sense of it all.

Liam and Cooper sit quietly, lost in their own thoughts. I can't help but feel like I should say something to Cooper—something more than just "thanks." But I don't know what. How do you thank someone for saving your world?

"Cooper," I gesture toward the back patio. He stands and follows me outside.

It's dark out here, but Olivia's string lights hang overhead, casting a warm glow over the covered patio. I walk over to her outdoor bar and stand behind it, leaning against the counter.

"Look," I start, "I just want to say thanks."

"You don't—" he begins, but I shake my head.

"No, I do. You didn't even hesitate, man. You killed someone for Maisie, and that's not something I take lightly. I know you're trained for this kind of thing—that it's part of the job. But today? That wasn't just a job. That was the love of my life... and you saved her. That's not small, Cooper."

He clears his throat. "I'll take that mark on my soul any day for the people I love. We're a family, and this past year's changed a lot for me. My perspective on life and family—on what really matters. I'm grateful for Drew and Hayes, for the opportunity to work with them... but it's not just about *brotherhood* anymore. We've got sisters, nieces, nephews—and even Connie and Zeke have been more parental to us than our own parents. So yeah, I appreciate it. But honestly? I wouldn't let anything happen to Maisie, or anyone else here."

"We feel the same about you guys, too." I spot a bottle of tequila sitting on the bar. Grabbing it, I set it down in front of us, then turn toward the shelf where Olivia keeps the shot glasses and pick out two.

Cooper watches me with a surprised look, then his mustache tugs to one side as he nods. "Got to say, I heard a rumor you got someone pregnant the last time you drank. Just so you know—I'm not into dudes."

I laugh. "Ha. You're definitely not my type." I start pouring, then raise the glass. "I'll never be able to repay Maisie for saving Jake, or you for saving her. But if you ever need anything, I'll do whatever I can to make sure you get it."

He lifts his shot. "To Maisie—and hopefully you knocking *her* up tonight," he says with a grin.

I can't help but laugh as I down my shot, feeling a little

lighter—if only for a moment. I quickly wash the glasses and we head back inside. Instinctively, I gravitate toward Maisie, who's leaning against the cabinets. She looks up at me and immediately gets on her tiptoes, pulling my face down to kiss me. When she pulls back, her eyes are wide—tasting the tequila—and she chuckles softly.

"Cooper! Is there anyone you haven't corrupted?" she teases, casting a playful glare in his direction.

He considers it for a second, then shrugs. "Only you, Maisie."

"Yeah, we'll keep it that way," I say with a fake stern look that, honestly, doesn't carry much weight.

"Fuck yeah!" Lincoln slams his hand down on the table, then shrinks back a little. "Sorry. But I fucking figured it out. CJ? His half-brother's Evan Johnson."

The realization hits me like a punch—Evan was the teammate I bought the card and baseball from. I quickly explain to everyone that Evan said it belonged to his dad, but he didn't "give a fuck about baseball." I've always been into collecting, and back then, he offered it to me for way less than it was worth. Under a million, that was close to seven or so years ago. I know the card's worth at least three now—and that doesn't even include the signed Mickey Mantle ball.

"First of all," Lincoln says, "that Evan guy? An idiot. But it makes sense CJ would be pissed he sold his dad's collector's items."

He pauses, then asks, "How the hell did he find Stephanie and get her involved?"

Maisie shrugs, hesitating before she says, "Odessa quickly realized that she was..." she trails off. Her gaze lingers on me a moment longer, silent but conveying her discomfort with calling Stephanie Jake's anything—let alone his biological mom.

She shakes her head slightly. "Anyway, if he was around

any of those parties, and she was there, or other people were around—it's not a secret that Ethan had a kid and moved back home. Just Google his name—hundreds of articles come up because it was such a crazy move."

"That's why Stephanie said it could be wired money or something worth three million," I add.

"Unless it was all a ruse—CJ's master plan, maybe," Delta suggests. "He'd been working for Ethan for months. No one takes such a minimum-wage job for that long without an ulterior motive."

Lincoln's expression tightens. "A guy nearly a hundred K in credit card debt would. Looks like Daddy Johnson didn't leave much to his new wife and kid—compared to what he left to his ex-wife and their kid. The divorce settlement? Seventy percent of his estate went to Evan."

"So," I say slowly, "he came after me, kidnapped Jake, threatened Maisie's life—because he wanted the payout?"

"I don't know, man," Lincoln admits, voice brisk. "But it's starting to look like you were kind of an easy target. He probably didn't realize what he was up against until he moved here. By then, his plan was already in motion."

"It still doesn't explain why Jason's involved," Margie says softly from her spot at the corner of the table.

Lincoln sighs heavily, wariness flickering in his eyes—like he's reluctant to tell her what he's about to.

"Marguerite," he begins, pronouncing it perfectly, as if he's hiding some flawless French accent we don't know about. "Do you—do you know if Jason has any addictions?"

She hesitates, her eyes on him. "I don't know. He takes... he has a lot of body aches from working so much."

"Pills?" Maisie asks gently, but I catch the shock in her voice. I squeeze her shoulder, offering silent support, and she relaxes into me again. I know Maisie didn't realize, and honestly, neither did I. A drinking problem? I could've guessed from how many times we had to call him an Uber or make sure he wasn't over served at the bar.

"Yeah," Margie nods, her lip starting to quiver. "Sometimes. The doctor prescribed them, though."

Lincoln probes softly, "Any other addictions?"

She looks at him, unsure. "Why?"

He hesitates. "Because I've found some threatening texts and missed calls. And I've tracked his location over the last few months. He's been spending a lot of time at the casino up north."

A ripple of shock runs through everyone, but we all stay quiet, letting Margie process it.

"Gambling debts? Like, he *owes* money to bad guys?"

Lincoln nods slowly. "Unfortunately... and... they're trying to collect."

She gasps, horror flickering across her face at the implication.

His arm slips around her, pulling her close. "We won't let anything happen to you or the kids."

Before any of us can say anything, the front door slams shut with a loud bang, and everyone jumps. Every guy except Lincoln is on their feet, poised and ready to pounce on whoever just walked in.

I shift, starting to pull Maisie behind me, but then I see it's Levi.

He's moving fast, his face tense, then raises his hands in a defensive gesture. "Shit. Sorry, the wind caught that," he mumbles quickly.

Behind him, two people trail inside, but he's blocking enough I can't quite tell who they are. A young woman with bright red hair—nothing fake or box-dyed, just a rich, eye-catching shade. She's probably in her mid-twenties. Right behind her, almost hidden, is a blonde kid about her height, but he couldn't be more than a teen, if that.

It isn't until Levi spots Maisie and starts moving toward us that I get a better look at the kid.

"Mais!" Levi throws his arms around her, then pulls back quickly, concern flickering across his face. "You okay?" he asks, his voice tight.

Maisie responds, but I don't even catch what she says—my focus is glued to the two strangers just a few feet in front of us.

Levi steps back, and I notice how his shoulder lines up with the top of the kid's head. I keep bouncing my gaze between them—the resemblance is uncanny. It's almost like—

"Holy *shit*," Maisie gasps. "You have a kid?!"

Epilogue

Maisie

Less than a month after the shooting, Ethan had the whole library cleaned up. The wall behind the pine painting was now a different color—still bright, but with a sense of a fresh start. He asked me if I wanted a new painting, but it didn't remind me of CJ, so I said no. The safe still sat there, quiet and unmoved, tucked away where it belongs. But I didn't want that one moment—the violence, the fear—to tarnish what I had built in this space. I can wholeheartedly say that my perfect library remained intact, cherished, and loved.

After the investigation wrapped up, we moved back in. Luke decided to ask the neighboring county to handle the cleanup and the legal aftermath, feeling he was too close to the situation, especially with Jason involved. As for Jason, he's still in jail, facing charges I don't fully understand the meaning of. Margie's doing her best to pick up the pieces, staying with our parents until they can figure out who Jason owes money to and how to handle that mess.

Despite everything, life pressed forward. And so today, I wanted to surprise Ethan with something just as meaningful.

No grand proposal—just us, in the backyard; a quiet, intimate celebration. Cooper, being the online ordained officiant—although I'd never quite trusted those sites completely—will be here, ready to perform the ceremony.

I hired Callie to be my event coordinator, and with her and Odessa's help, the yard was transformed into a dream. Flowers —all kinds—colored every inch. Peonies, daisies, lavender, and wildflowers created a fragrant tapestry that fluttered in the breeze.

An elegant wooden arch, dressed with cascading greenery and more blooms, stood at the center, overlooking the rolling green fields that had always been my sanctuary.

This evening, the sun will dip below the horizon, casting a warm, golden glow, as twinkle lights begin to sparkle and illuminate the yard with a gentle shimmer. I'll marry the best friend I've ever had and become a mom to the child I've only loved from afar. *I can't wait!*

Currently, the men are picking up the tuxes that Odessa ordered custom for them. I don't know how she played it off, but somehow that woman worked her magic and all the guys went to pick up the new tailored ware that she insisted every man should have. Ethan is still oblivious to what is going on, but Jake knows, and he pinky promised he wouldn't tell his dad. I put a lot of faith in a six-year-old, but I trust that little guy more than I trust most adults.

Little did Ethan know, when he left this morning, I had a full glam squad on their way—Charlie's recommendation had us all primped and polished, getting ready together. We picked out my dress last week: a romantic satin ball gown with a deep V-neck. It was off-the-rack, but it fit like it was made for me. That gown, with its flowing fabric and delicate pleats, made me feel like I stepped straight out of a fairytale. Which, I kind of did.

I step into the kitchen where my sister Margie, my friends Charlie, Isla, and Odessa are gathered. Margie is fussing with a hairpin, Charlie adjusting her makeup mirror, Isla smoothing out her sleeves, and Odessa scrolling through her phone—each of them glowing with excitement. Off to the side, Olivia sits peacefully in a rocking chair, cradling her two-week-old newborn, quietly watching everything unfold, her expression tender and proud.

Meanwhile, Ellie is off in a corner on a play mat, happily playing with August, their giggles filling the air. It's chaotic and beautiful all at once—a whirlwind of love, anticipation, and tiny moments of joy.

Suddenly, all heads snap up as the room falls silent, and my gaze lands on their faces—it's the waterworks, the suffocating gushing of emotion, and the gasps that confirm how beautiful I felt looking in the bathroom mirror.

My mom steps up last, her eyes misty but shining. "You look incredible," she whispers, her voice thick with pride.

"Thanks, mama," I whisper back, my voice trembling. For whatever reason, tears fill my eyes — overwhelmed by the love, the moment, and the journey that brought us here.

"You deserve to have the best future with Ethan," she says, gently squeezing my hand. "No matter how long it took you to get here, you're here now, and that's what matters."

I take a deep breath, feeling the warmth of everyone's love surrounding me, knowing that today is turning out exactly how I always hoped it could be.

There's no way to hide the setup, so as soon as Hayes texts that he's passing my parents' place, I step out the front door to wait. He'll see the flowers from the gate, but at least he won't see me in the dress until they drive up the hill and around the corner. I take a deep breath, trying to steady my nerves, feeling the weight of the moment settle over me.

Hayes's truck pulls around the bend, its engine rumbling softly on the gravel. Before it even comes to a stop, the back door swings open with a flourish, and Ethan is jumping out with that familiar, eager energy.

"Holy shit! My Beautiful Bride Maisie!" His grin is so wide it's contagious as he runs toward me with open arms. His eyes shimmer with excitement and affection. "What is happening?"

"Surprise?" I manage, a shaky laugh escaping as he barrels into me, wrapping his arms around me so tightly I almost stumble.

"You look... There aren't even words, Maisie," he whispers, the emotion thick in his voice, a sniffle behind his breath betraying his efforts to stay composed.

"I don't want to wait. Or do the whole proposal, stress about a wedding," I admit, voice trembling with anticipation. "I just want to marry you. Here. Right now. Is that okay?"

His eyes catch mine, shining bright with love and certainty. "Are you kidding me? There isn't a single day in my life I wouldn't have married you—yesterday, today, or ten years from now. I'd wait for you for a lifetime, Maisie."

So underneath that beautiful floral arch, with just a small circle of friends and family, Ethan and I exchanged vows that felt like the culmination of everything—the pain, the hope, the love that had carried us through it all. No fancy sermons, or overly dramatic speeches—just honest words and quiet promises. And when I looked into Ethan's eyes, I just knew that all those years without each other were worth it. Because in that backyard, on our hill, my dream finally came true.

Already ready for more Cascadia County? Read on for a sneak peek of Book 6 in The Cascadia County Series—Behind the Wildflowers.

Behind the Wildflowers

Prologue

Levi—age 20

Cruising toward Bend, the sunset paints the mountains gold—kind of how I feel inside: nervous, excited, scared, but mostly thrilled. Summer's long days make the late drive feel natural, almost timeless.

The only thing on my mind is Sienna—my newly established girlfriend that I can't seem to get enough of—her laugh, her intelligence. She's got this dark red hair that reminds me of the natural garnet necklace my mom used to wear—deep, rich, and shining with understated elegance. It was the first thing I noticed about her, like my mom was sending me a message saying, *This is it. She could be the one.* She's shorter than me, but about average in height, and those hazel-green eyes—God, her eyes—so full of life. Needless to say, I'm falling for her, falling hard and fast.

Last-minute, she invited me over tonight, and I jumped at

the chance to spend time with her. I live for these rare moments —those few hours a week we get together—that make all the busy days worth it. We're both students at the community college in Bend—me studying paramedicine, her for dental assisting—and we are both working full-time.

We've only been dating a few months, and she just dropped a bomb on me: she's pregnant.

The road blurs, and suddenly, I'm transported back to a few weeks ago.

We're sitting in my truck, just the two of us, parked in the trees on the edge of campus. It's the beginning of summer, birds chirping, and the warm sunlight filtering through the leaves. It should've been our little break from everything else, but from the moment she got in, I could tell something was off simply by looking at her face. She doesn't beat around the bush, though. First thing she says is, "I'm pregnant."

Everything in me stills for a second as I scan her face, trying to figure out if she's joking or serious. Fear hits me first—like a punch out of nowhere, with the how's, why's, and holy shit's racing through my head. But once I snap out of it, I see her shoulders softly shaking. Then I notice tears starting to stream down her face. Without thinking, I pull her close, rub her back, trying to make sense of everything.

"Hey, hey," I whisper, my voice steady despite all the chaos going on inside. "It's okay. We'll figure this out."

Only my words bounce back at me, like they aren't even registering with her. She starts crying harder, clutching her stomach, devastation pouring out of her as if this is the worst news possible. I don't get her reaction, though. Yeah, it's not what I was expecting, but that doesn't mean it's bad news.

"Are you... are you mad at me?" she asks, her voice breaking through tears.

"No, Sienna. Never. I—" My voice catches. "Why would I be mad at you?"

She looks at me, eyes red and desperate. "I didn't mean for this to happen, Levi, I swear. I've been on birth control... I don't even know how far along I might be—"

"Hey, it's okay," I cut her off softly. "We'll figure out all the details. A doctor will know for sure."

She nods, still trembling. "I just... I haven't been with anyone for over a year, Levi. I swear. It's yours."

Realization dawns on me. She thought I'd have an entirely different reaction— accuse her, blame the situation on her, whatever else douchebags do in situations like this.

I squeeze her hand. "The baby not being mine wasn't even a thought. We're in this together. You, me, the baby."

We try to do some math, guessing how far along she could be, but she keeps shaking her head. Turns out she's been taking birth control the whole time, which makes things even more confusing.

She sniffles, then looks at me anxiously. "Will the baby be okay? Like, is birth control somehow poisoning it?"

God, I want to tell her she doesn't have to worry about that. My knowledge might be limited as a paramedic-to-be, but I know this: I want this little one.

"I don't know," I say softly.

"What if I've been hurting him or her?" she asks, voice trembling again.

I want to reassure her, but all I can do is shrug. "We'll make an appointment, first thing, and they'll make sure the baby is healthy. Okay? One step at a time."

She looks over, biting her lip. "Do you think your family will hate me?"

"No! Dan's going to be mad I beat him to the punch, but he'll be happy if I'm happy." That's the thing about twins—we may fight over anything we can, but when it comes down to it, there isn't anyone I trust more than him. Womb mates, roommates, and now the best mates. Or whatever the saying is.

She nods. "And your dad? What about my mom? They're both going to freak out."

That thought stops the memory cold, and I have to shake it off and refocus on the road. I don't know how my dad will feel about me becoming a dad so young and out of wedlock. I do know my dad's a good man—the sheriff of this little town, the kind of guy everyone trusts. He'll want me to step up and be there, no matter what. But I'm pretty sure my recent mess hasn't been sitting well with him. If anything, I think this little accident will only prove I'm not.

Last month, I lost it. Caught some lowlife trying to sexually assault a friend of mine. I didn't just get angry—I saw red. Almost killed the guy, but Sienna stopped me. My knuckles still sting from the punches thrown, but I'd do it again in a heartbeat.

And the trouble with her mom? Yeah, that's a whole other story. She's a nurse at the hospital, was working on the guy I beat up—and refused to talk to me afterward. Said I wasn't good enough for Sienna. Maybe I'm not.

I'm still a student, working crazy hours as an EMT, although I'm almost done. Once I pass my exam, I'll be able to get licensed. With any luck, that'll be a couple of months before the baby is born. *Is that enough time? Can we handle a new relationship, new job, and a newborn?*

I run a hand through my hair, trying to breathe.

"Stop," I command into the silence. "Sienna is safe and healthy. That's all that matters. Everything else will work itself out."

After a few moments, Sienna's voice echoes in my head— soft and determined— and I'm back that day, listening to her gush about our baby.

"I already love this little one," she admits. "My mom will get over it. I know you have a good heart. It'll just take time."

I zone in on her words. "You already love it?"

She nods, looks at me with that little sparkle in her eyes, and says, "Is that crazy? I just keep imagining a little boy that looks just like you."

I can't help but preen a little at the thought, feeling a smile tug on my lips. Honestly, imagining that feels... right. As if it's meant to be. But then something else sneaks in, and I can't stop myself from saying it: "Or a little girl who looks just like you."

Her smile widens, and she leans her head on my shoulder. I can see she's already picturing it—the tiny baby with dark red hair and her hazel eyes.

"Wait," she says, her voice a little playful. "What about names? There are so many to pick from!"

"Well... uhm, if it's a boy, he has to be named Cal."

Her eyebrows shoot up. "Why?"

"I may have made a promise in high school—I'd name my firstborn son after Mr. Calvin. He gave me enough extra credit to bump my grade from a high B to a low A...

and I promised him I'd name my first kid after him if he did it."

"You're joking!" She looks at me like I'm crazy, but when she sees I'm not, she smiles anyway.

I tap my fingers on her shoulders, rhythmically. "No, Sienna, this isn't a joking matter." I try to say as seriously as I can. "It was *very* important to me to get straight A's throughout high school."

"Seriously?" she asks, cracking up.

"Yeah," I say, shrugging. "I was always kind of competitive about grades. Dan was the goodie-two-shoes—the one who never got into trouble. I was known as 'the troublemaker,' but I still made sure my GPA was better than his. Plus, that meant my dad couldn't complain much because I was always bringing home good grades."

She chuckles softly and leans against me. "That's actually... surprisingly endearing."

"Baby Cal—you okay with that?"

She pauses thoughtfully, then glances at me, a little teasing. "Sure, but what about a girl? Did you sign your soul away for that name, too?"

I burst out laughing. "No—I'm open to anything. Whatever feels right."

Her eyes soften again, and she nods. "Me too."

A beat of silence, then she looks at me, like she's gathering her courage. "Levi, I know this all happens so suddenly, and it's a lot to take in... but if I have to go through it with anyone, I'm really glad it's you."

H er words hit me right in the chest that day. There are a lot of women in the world I could never imagine raising a child with, but Sienna isn't one of them. She's light, warm, full of energy and smiles— but above all else, she's kind.

I pull into a parking space outside her apartment, excited to see her. The doctor appointment we went to last week said she was measuring around twenty-one weeks, which means she got pregnant pretty much the first time we had sex. Not ideal by any circumstances, but it makes sense. She's barely showing, which is actually the reason she took a test to begin with. At first, she thought she was bloated from the new birth control pills, and they were causing the weird symptoms she was having. But no—somehow, the timeline didn't work out. From when she thought she'd be protected to us having sex, it didn't add up. Add to that she was skipping the "sugar pills," experiencing occasional breakthrough bleeding—or what she thought was breakthrough bleeding—and here we are.

We opted to wait on finding out the gender; she wants to be surprised. But I'd be lying if I said I wasn't looking at that ultrasound wishing I knew how to read it.

Either way, she has the cutest little bump that I find my hand gravitating toward anytime we are together.

I make my way to the first-floor apartment she lives in, paid for by her dad, who's a surgeon in California. It seems as if they don't have much of a relationship, but beyond the basics, she avoids talking about him. It's a nice little one-bedroom, but I'm hoping I can convince her to move to Three Sisters with me. I already called a family friend— Lovey, who owns most of the rentals in Central Oregon— and asked if she had anything available. She's setting me up with a modest two-bedroom house on the outskirts of town.

My knuckles rap on the door, a smile spreading on my face. I genuinely like Sienna, and although this is a confusing time, spending time with her is the best. She's funny and light-hearted, making jokes that are funnier than most of my friends.

Even Dan likes her— thinks she's a good fit to match my energy. Which says a lot, considering I don't think he's ever liked a girl I've brought home.

After a minute of her not answering, I knock again and step back. She texted me less than thirty minutes ago and said she was excited to see me, so I know she's here. I tune my ears to listen inside, but there's nothing on the other side of the door. When she still doesn't come out, I pull out my phone and hit the call button.

Dread hits me instantly when I hear it ringing on the other side. My fist pounds on the door, worry hitting me like a freight train.

She still doesn't come.

I try for the handle and with ease it opens, but what I never expected to see is Sienna on the floor, lying on her side.

I run to her, dropping to my knees immediately. My training takes over. I check her responsiveness—no reaction. Her eyes are dilated, skin warm and clammy. She's unresponsive, no pulse. My heart races— I dial 911 and start CPR, pushing hard, fast.

"911..."

"Medical emergency, pregnant woman found unconscious at the Stone Butte Apartment Complex, #104."

Dispatch relays instructions, telling me to stay calm, but I'm in the zone. My focus shifts from her chest to her open mouth.

Come on, Levi. Stay focused. Save her.

I lose track of time—maybe a minute, maybe five. The crew arrives behind me, and I keep pumping.

"Turner?" I don't have to look to recognize Josiah's voice. I've trained as much as I could over the last few years with Deschutes County Fire and Rescue, as well as worked in my own neighboring county, Cascadia.

I repeat what I told dispatch, never losing rhythm, even though sweat drips from my brow. "Unresponsive when I arrived, found her here, 22 weeks pregnant…"

His hand grips my shoulder, relieving me from my duty so they can take over, but I don't want to stop.

"We've got it, son. You can ride—let's go."

I fall back on my haunches and let them work. Within a minute, they have her loaded, and I'm in the captain's seat as they continue treatment. Josiah is operating the LUCAS chest compression device, and I can only watch from what feels like a distance beyond my body's reach— as if I've hoisted myself above the chaos, observing the scene with a detached clarity that's almost surreal.

Her heart is beating on its own by the time we arrive at the hospital, but she's still not awake. Barely breathing, but she made it—that's all I can focus on.

They take her behind the doors, and I'm left standing in the waiting room, feeling numb. My body remains still, in shock from what just happened, but somehow I manage to sit.

Right when I'm about to ask for an update, a mane of red hair pulled into a sleek bun bursts out of the ICU doors. I recognize her immediately—Sienna's mom.

Anger and pain radiate from her body, and when she sets her sights on me, I know it's all going to be directed at me.

"Get the fuck out! You don't belong here!" she screams.

I stand up, my hands rising in a plea. "I didn't—"

"You did! That baby caused a P.E., and it's your fault she's pregnant!"

"P.E.?" It hits me—pulmonary embolism. It can cause sudden cardiac arrest and stop her heart, or severe hypoxia, depriving the brain of oxygen. She'd have been gone by the time I got there. Nothing I could've done would have saved her.

But— her heart was beating again in the ambulance. I saw it with my own two eyes.

"She's gone! Because of you, she's as good as dead!" Her fists hit my chest, and I don't even care that it hurts. I'm still reeling from her words.

"As good as dead? But—the baby," I say, disbelief thick in my voice, as a security guard approaches, wrapping his arms around her and pulling her back.

"You killed them." Her last words echo in my mind. I fall to my knees, my body shuddering with disbelief. *Did I really do this? Is this my fault?*

Also by TJ Deal

The Cascadia County Series

Behind the Cascades

Behind the Juniper

Behind the Larch

Behind the Yarrow

Behind the Pine

Behind the Wildflowers

About the Author

TJ Deal is a Pacific Northwest-based aspiring author who often daydreams about writing stories in the incredible places she travels to around the world. Thanks to her husband's unwavering support and her lifelong obsession with reading, she has decided to follow her passion for writing. Her days are mostly spent drinking coffee, relishing in the daily grind of motherhood, and capitalizing on every free moment to work on her latest novel.